The
Other
Side
of
Free

This book is dedicated to
the people who built Fort Mose,
those who fought for her,
and those who've made sure their story is told.
—K.R.

Ω

Published by
PEACHTREE PUBLISHERS
1700 Chattahoochee Avenue
Atlanta, Georgia 30318-2112

www.peachtree-online.com

Text © 2013 by Krista Russell

Cover illustration by Tom Gonzalez
Cover design by Loraine Joyner
Book design by Melanie McMahon Ives

Manufactured in August 2013 by RR Donnelley & Sons in Harrisonburg, Viriginia, in the United States of America
10 9 8 7 6 5 4 3 2 1
First edition

Russell, Krista.
The other side of free / by Krista Russell.
    pages cm
  Summary: In 1739, having escaped from slavery under the British, thirteen-year-old Jem finds himself in the custody of sharp-tongued Phaedra at Fort Mose in Spanish Florida, but his efforts to break free of Phaedra's will have surprising results.
ISBN-13: 978-1-56145-710-6
ISBN-10: 1-56145-710-8
[1. Fugitive slaves—Fiction. 2. African Americans—Fiction. 3. Underground Railroad—Fiction. 4. Slavery—Fiction. 5. Spaniards—Florida—Fiction. 6. Fort Mose Site (Fla.)—Fiction. 7. Florida—History—Spanish colony, 1565-1763—Fiction.] I. Title.
PZ7.R915454Oth 2013
[Fic]—dc23
                         2012050989

The
Other
Side
of
Free

KRISTA RUSSELL

PEACHTREE
ATLANTA

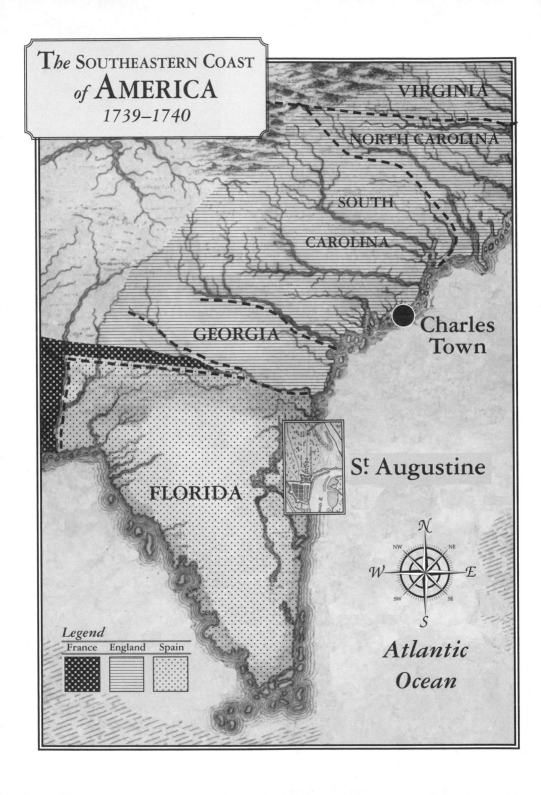

The SOUTHEASTERN COAST
of AMERICA
1739–1740

VIRGINIA

NORTH CAROLINA

SOUTH

CAROLINA

GEORGIA

Charles
Town

FLORIDA

St Augustine

Legend
France England Spain

N
NW NE
W E
SW SE
S

Atlantic
Ocean

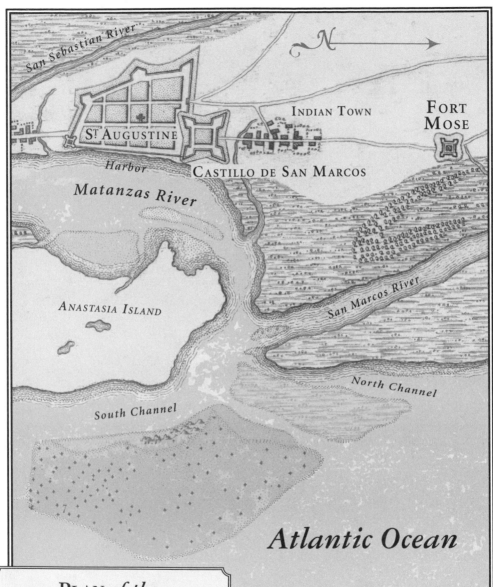

San Sebastian River

N

St Augustine

Indian Town

Fort Mose

Harbor

Castillo de San Marcos

Matanzas River

Anastasia Island

San Marcos River

North Channel

South Channel

Atlantic Ocean

Plan *of the* **Town** *and* **Harbor** *of* **St Augustine** and **Surroundings** *1739–1740*

CHARLES TOWN
FEBRUARY 16, 1739

R ise up!" Aunt Winnie's whisper was low and insistent. Jem
tried to cover his head with the worn rice sacks he used as
blankets. The night was shivery and the root cellar smelled
of damp. Bright lamplight shone in his eyes.

"Boy looks sickly," a woman said. "You sure he ain't got the
fever?"

Jem came awake at the sound of the unfamiliar voice. He was
dimly aware that it must be very late, for the stone Aunt Winnie
had warmed for his bed was cold against his feet.

"Needs some fresh air and greens is all," Aunt Winnie said. The
lantern clanked as she set it on a barrel.

"You told me he was thirteen! Don't look half that."

"You backing out?"

"Too late for that. But I should've looked at the boy before I
bargained with you, old woman. This runt ain't good for nothing.
Can't even get himself up."

The pallet was yanked out from under Jem and he landed hard
on the dirt floor.

"Quick now." Aunt Winnie pulled him to his feet.

He squinted at the dark-skinned woman standing next to her.
With a long neck sticking out of her cloak and a black wrap around

her head, the woman reminded him of a buzzard. Her bony claws clutched at his pallet.

"This here's Phaedra," Aunt Winnie said to Jem. "You're going with her."

"Going where?" His voice was a squeak. What was she talking about? Jem shook his head, but couldn't clear the confusion. "Are you coming?" he asked. Jem didn't like the look of the stranger. He wouldn't go anywhere with her unless Aunt Winnie came, too.

Aunt Winnie spit into the darkness. "Never mind where. I'll be along later." She grasped his chin. Her fingers were warm and smelled of sassafras and pokeberry, sharp but also soothing, like Aunt Winnie herself. Even in the shadowy light, he could make out the dark red stain around her nails. "Promise me you'll do as she says."

Jem glanced back at the younger woman. Something glinted like cold steel in the opening of her cloak—a silver medallion.

"You must give me your vow." Aunt Winnie raised his chin so she was looking deep into his eyes.

He stared back at her, his resolve evaporating like morning mist over the Cooper River. It was impossible to deny Aunt Winnie. Though not his blood, she was the closest thing to family he'd ever known.

She was also Charles Town's most powerful conjure woman. And Jem knew better than to resist the forces of conjuration.

"I promise," he whispered.

Chapter One

Spanish Florida
October 13, 1739

The fort was eerily quiet. Shadows hung like phantoms in the dark reaches of the yard. Most of the militia had gone to the Castillo de San Marco, the large fortress in St. Augustine. A small group sat around the fire. Big Sunday, who'd been one of the first to escape to Florida, had taken his usual place at the center of the gathering. His half-Indian son, Domingo, had come from his village toting a string of fish he'd speared in the harbor.

"Tell a tale about Brother Rabbit," Jem said, thinking of the story Aunt Winnie had told him the night he left Charles Town. He'd puzzled over its meaning all the long months he'd been in Spanish Florida.

"Which one?" Big Sunday asked. He stoked the fire with a long stick, releasing a swirl of fiery embers into the moon-lit sky.

"The one where he tricks Fox into leading him out of the Great Dismal." Jem shivered at the images the swamp's name conjured: water the color of tobacco spit, tree cover so thick it blocked all daylight, and winding trails that led nowhere. No telling what manner of wild beast lurked within.

Phaedra snorted. "We'd be better off if we'd gone to the Dismal instead of coming here."

Evenings at Fort Mose hadn't been the same since Phaedra started sitting up late with the others. She'd broken the magic of the circle, ruined the spell of the stories. There were almost a hundred people living at the fort, and dozens used to come to listen to Big Sunday's stories. Now most retired early, and those who stayed were quiet, wary of Phaedra's sharp tongue.

"I'd rather face the English across a battlefield than live like an animal in the swamp," Big Sunday said.

Phaedra grunted. "You think we're any different from those critters in your stories? No sir, the Spanish got us stuck out here like rabbits in a trap."

Jem touched the blue beads Aunt Winnie had sewn onto his shirt. He was glad he had them to protect him. "Brother Rabbit wouldn't let himself get caught," he said, hoping Big Sunday would tell the tale.

"Nobody asked you. Make yourself useful and fetch my shawl." Phaedra kept her eyes on the sweetgrass basket she was working on. Her fingers snatched at the fronds again and again, until each strip was bent and shaped to her will.

Jem left the fire and made his way across the yard toward the thatched hut where they slept. But when he entered the dark *chosa*, he stubbed his toe on a bedpost. Hopping on his other foot, Jem fought the urge to cry out. Phaedra was always going on about how clumsy he was. Finally, the pain became a dull throb. He dropped to his knees and drew a circle in the dirt. Through the middle, he marked an X. He spit onto the center and walked slowly around the circle. Satisfied he'd countered the bad luck, Jem smoothed the dirt and crept carefully around the gloomy hut until he found Phaedra's shawl.

"Took you long enough," she said when he returned to the fire. "You get lost?"

Someone laughed. Jem scanned the faces, but couldn't tell who. He decided to ignore Phaedra's remark. Keeping his eyes on the ground, he went back to his whittling. But it was as though the whistle were made of straw. His knife sliced too deeply into the stick, breaking it in half. He threw the remnants into the fire and watched them catch and burn.

A twig snapped outside the circle and Shadrack stepped into the light. "Something out there," he announced.

Shadrack was the oldest of the escaped slaves who'd made their way south to freedom. Maroons, the Spanish called them. The old man slept in the woods beside the kiln where he burned the wood to make the charcoal needed to forge weapons for the militia. But he came to Fort Mose for meals. He wore brown trousers and a tunic turned gray from soot. His watery eyes seemed unnaturally wide, likely because his lashes and brows had been singed off so many times they'd given up growing back.

"What'd you see?" Big Sunday barked, the rich cadence of his storytelling voice gone like smoke.

"Not see." Shadrack tapped a finger to the side of his grizzled head. "Hear."

"Only thing you ever hear is the dinner bell," Thomas the blacksmith said.

"Then tell us what you heard," Big Sunday ordered.

"Nothing."

Phaedra snickered.

Shadrack turned to her, his voice dropping to a whisper. "When *obia* come, the critters go still."

The flesh on Jem's arm prickled. He traced a finger along the hem of his shirt where Aunt Winnie had sewn the line of blue beads to ward off the evil eye. He listened for the familiar sounds of the night from outside the fort's earthen walls, but heard only the crackle of the fire.

A log fell, sending sparks flying.

Jem started and then stole a glance to the side, hoping Domingo hadn't seen him flinch. Big Sunday's son made him uneasy. More than once he'd snuck up on Jem in the forest, or appeared suddenly beside him as he gathered grass in the marsh. Domingo had an air of watchful stealth that reminded Jem of the sly trickster, Brother Fox.

"Leave off with your stories," Phaedra said. "I've had my fill. If it's not you bending our ears with your African mumbo jumbo, it's that priest going on about Daniel and the lion and such. Truth telling's what we need here in purgatory, not tall tales!"

Shadrack shook his head. "I feel sorry for all you this-country-born folk. You'll change your mind when obia come for you." He glanced at Jem. "Or mayhap he come for your little brother."

Jem jumped to his feet. "I'm not her brother!" He glared at the faces around the circle. They didn't understand. Most of them had kin. He had no one. Not since Aunt Winnie had traded him off like a sack of rice.

Phaedra ignored him. "Don't waste your pity on me, old man," she told Shadrack. "I was born kicking. Anything comes for me, I'll be ready."

"So will I!" Jem said, jumping up and overturning the basket Phaedra had been working on.

Phaedra snatched up the basket and glared at him. "What you gonna do?" she scoffed. "Whistle at them?"

"I can take care of myself."

"You can't take care of nothing," she said. "Almost killed the whole flock of chickens when you let the water run out."

"I didn't!" he cried. He was sure he'd filled that water bowl. "You probably kicked it over yourself!"

"Hush now, boy," Big Sunday said. "Show some respect."

The wind changed, and a fetid smell filled the clearing.

Big Sunday grimaced. "What in creation?" he asked, turning toward Shadrack.

The old man held out a leather pouch on a hide string tied around his neck. "Conjure bag. Just got it. Keep obia away."

Phaedra fanned the air in front of her nose. "Obia's not all it'll keep away."

"Don't mind her," Jem told Shadrack. "She don't know about the powers of conjuration." He turned toward the fire, away from the smell. Of this he was certain: there were mighty forces at work in the world. Unseen, yet irresistible. A trick, a charm, or a curse, and life could change in a hair's breadth. Conjure was a way to right wrongs, a way to even the scales.

"Shut your mouth and fetch more firewood," Phaedra said.

Jem ground his toes into the packed dirt, then rose to obey. He'd had his fill of doing Phaedra's bidding. If only Aunt Winnie hadn't made him promise. Her betrayal stuck in the back of his throat, like a swallow of rancid stew that refused to stay down. He collected more logs from the wood-pile and placed them carefully on the fire.

He'd kept his word, hadn't he? He'd followed Phaedra into the night and away from Master's house, followed her past the taverns on the waterfront to the docks, and followed her right into the hold of the leaky ship that carried them to freedom in Florida. Except being here didn't feel like freedom.

He was almost fourteen now. Old enough to be his own master. Old enough to join the militia. Yet Phaedra still treated him like a child, incapable of performing the simplest chore without mishap. Breaking free of her wouldn't be easy. It would take all his wits and maybe a strong dose of conjure. But he was ready.

Big Sunday peered out at the walls of the fort as though he might see right through them into the forest. "Could be English spies out there. Or scouts. Just thirty-five miles between us and their troops."

"Let obia take them all." Phaedra picked out a line of her weaving with her horn nail, a spoon with the bowl removed and the end sharpened to a point. Jem ran his hands over his forearms, conscious of the times he'd felt the jab of that horn nail when he didn't move as quickly as she liked.

Big Sunday turned back to the fire. "We swore an oath to fight the English."

Phaedra's laugh was harsh. "We vowed to stand betwixt two bands of white men intent on killing each other. I say we step out of the way and let them commence."

"And if the English win, you're content to be a slave again?" Big Sunday asked her.

Phaedra frowned. "How many years were you in St. Augustine before the Spanish remembered their promise of freedom? Ten? Eleven? The Spanish don't take pains to remember their oaths. You don't need to remind me about mine."

Jem glanced over at Domingo. Had he taken the oath? Jem couldn't picture it. Domingo had a crafty smugness about him that made it seem unlikely he'd make many promises, let alone keep them. Why did he live at the Indian village instead of here with his pa? With his ma gone, what reason could there be, other than that he was afraid of the English?

Well, Jem wasn't afraid. In the months he'd been at the fort, he'd learned his way around every pine barren, palmetto scrub, and oak grove outside its walls. "I'll go," he said. In the silence that followed, the rashness of his words came down on him like a cane whip. What if there really was a fearsome obia out there?

"Go where?" Big Sunday asked.

Brandishing his whittling knife, Jem pointed toward the forest. The solid weight of the handle reassured him. "See what's out there."

"You'll do no such thing." Phaedra shook her head. "Only a fool would go out into the night because of what another fool didn't hear in the woods."

"She's right," Big Sunday said.

With both of them against him, no good would come of arguing.

A lone star blazed a trail across the dark sky. Jem recognized it at once. It was just the sign he needed. He might be small, but he was clever. And he knew to take care in the forest.

"Then I'm going to bed," he said. As he turned to leave, his eyes met Domingo's. An odd expression crossed the older boy's face, disappearing in a trice.

He knows something, Jem decided as the fire's comforting glow faded behind him. *Does he suspect what I'm planning to do?*

Then another thought struck him hard.

Maybe he knows what's out there.

Chapter Two

October 13, 1739

Jem headed toward his chosa, then ducked behind the well and doubled back past the watchtower, out of sight of both the fire and the huts. The moon shone high in the autumn sky, signaling that it was already past ten o'clock.

As he approached the wall, Jem couldn't help pondering what Phaedra had said about the fort being a trap. How could a few logs piled with earth be enough to keep the English, or anyone else, out? Yet they must. Fort Mose was built to protect St. Augustine from the English. It was what all who lived there had sworn to do.

All except Jem. Phaedra wouldn't let him take the oath when they'd arrived. She'd said he was too young to be held accountable. The shame of it still burned his cheeks.

He touched the handle of his knife and started up the sloped earthen wall that surrounded Mose. He'd discovered the secret pathway early in his days at the fort—found it when Phaedra sent him to forage for the long grasses, pine needles, and palmetto fronds she needed for her baskets. Jem was proud that he could now come and go as he pleased, without having to report to the sentry at the gate. The forest had become his sanctuary; he found refuge under the wide canopies of oak hung with moss and comfort in the clean smell of crushed sassafras leaves.

But he'd never gone into the woods after dark.

At the top of the wall he turned back to gaze across the yard. It wasn't much of a fortress, really. Not like the one in Charles Town or the Castillo in St. Augustine. Fort Mose only had one cannon, and there were no stone bastions, no gun deck, and no drawbridge. Still, it had its own sort of grandness. It rose out of the earth from which it was cut, built of pine and cypress, mud and palm from the forest and marshes.

Maybe he saw it that way because he'd helped build Fort Mose, gathering oyster shells for the tabby and sticks and vines for the wattle and daub. He'd patted mud to form the walls of the very chosa where he should now be sleeping.

Outside the fort, there was only darkness. Two miles to the south, St. Augustine slept. Clouds had drifted in, obscuring the moonlight. Jem clutched at the wall, not wanting to let go of its solid safety.

When the clouds parted for a moment, the fields, forest, and creek appeared again as if by conjure. He touched the blue beads on his shirttail and swung over the top. Using the familiar footholds, he climbed down.

Jem only allowed himself a moment to glance to either side. Seeing no movement, he set out through the prickly palm that filled the ditch around the fort. Sharp fronds bit at his ankles and he wished he'd brought the machete he used to cut marsh grass and rushes for Phaedra's baskets.

He took care to feed his anger at her, knowing that if it fled, fear might worm its way in to fill the hole. Why, he should be on the gun deck of the Castillo right now with the rest of the Mose militia. Its thick stone bastions loomed large in his imagination, towering over the harbor and guarding St. Augustine. He might be smaller than the others, but some of them weren't much older. He should be with them, learning to fire a musket.

If Phaedra had her way he'd probably be perched next to her, sewing baskets. What he wouldn't do to shake free of that woman's bony grip!

Emerging from the ditch, Jem swatted at the swarm of mosquitoes gathering around his head and glanced toward St. Augustine. A sulfurous smell wafted in on the briny tang of the tide. Gunpowder? Jem imagined what it would be like to stand high on the Castillo's rampart looking out over the bay, a tricorn hat perched on his head and a musket at the ready. He could almost hear the hiss of the fuse and feel the cannon's deafening boom.

The sooner he proved himself, the better. If there was an English spy in the forest, Jem would find him. Then Phaedra would have to allow him to take his rightful place in the militia.

A cornfield was all that stood between him and the forest. The late crop was being left to dry before it was harvested for the winter stores. Husks and stalks would be fodder for the animals; cobs, fuel for the smudge pits. The sweet smell reminded him how long it had been since supper.

It had been his plan to find a tree he could climb to get

a better look around, but he hadn't accounted for how dark it would be in the woods.

And quiet.

Shadrack had been right; Jem could hear no signs of life within the forest. No birds, no crickets, no tree frogs. By contrast, every twig he stepped on cracked like musket fire. Even his breathing sounded unnaturally loud. Had Shadrack been right? Was there an evil spirit lurking in the night?

Jem shook himself. He was grown now, not the child he'd been in Charles Town. And a man soon to join the militia didn't quake in his boots. Besides, he had the beads to protect him.

Forging ahead, he stayed alert for any sound or sign of movement in the trees, but tried to focus on the familiar smells of the forest—the clean scent of pine, the earthy smell of the soil, the salty breeze carried from the marsh.

He'd walked for about a quarter of an hour when he heard it.

Smack, smack, smack. Like sticks banging together. Jem jumped at the sound, and turned so quickly that a tree branch brushed across his face. He swiped at it with one hand, and drew his knife with the other. He went completely still, except for the pounding in his chest.

The banging stopped. He forced himself to take a breath.

Inching away from the tree, he peered in the direction of the noise.

Twigs snapped behind him and Jem turned, but he could see nothing in the shadows. He waited, trying to convince himself it was the wind in the trees. When that didn't work, he told himself it was only Domingo, sneaking up on him again.

"Domingo?" he called. "That you?"

Silence.

"Stop fooling!"

There was a whoosh of air and something sharp and painful struck him hard on the back. He heard a roar as he pitched forward and went down, meeting the ground with a thud.

Next thing he knew, something had him by the shoulder and was turning him over. He tried to scream, but no sound came.

Jem stared up at the shadowy figure looming over him.

Then all was dark.

⚬

"He dead?" a soft voice whispered.

A searing heat burned Jem's eyelids.

"Naw, he's coming round."

Pine needles poked through the back of his shirt. When he moved, pain shot through his back and shoulder. He opened his eyes, but the light was too bright. Jem sat up and edged away from it, until his burning back hit something solid. He gasped, but it was only the trunk of a pine tree. He squinted, trying to see beyond the torch.

A woman bent over him.

"Aunt Winnie?" *She'd come for him!* His eyes filled and relief washed through his veins.

A man's voice came from behind the light. "Boy's talking nonsense."

The woman stood and Jem realized with a start that she wasn't Aunt Winnie. She was younger, though it was hard to tell her age. Her face was swollen and covered with insect bites. Instead of a long skirt, she wore baggy trousers. A cloth was wrapped around her neck and midsection; within it, something shifted and made a soft cry. She had a baby.

"Have we made it?" the man demanded.

"Made it where?" Jem asked, struggling to make sense of what had happened. He'd heard of witches turning into creatures to attack folks, but never while carrying a baby.

"To free," the woman said.

Jem's head cleared and he understood. They were maroons, looking for Mose. "You gave me a turn. I thought you…" He tried to stand, but stumbled.

The man helped him to his feet. "Are we near?"

"You could have just asked"—Jem tried to keep the vexation out of his voice—"instead of coming up on me like you did." He touched the spot on his shoulder, and then gazed at his hand. "You drew blood!"

"Boy," the man said gently, "you was out cold when we came upon you."

It didn't signify. "But I saw you."

"Not me."

"Nor me," said the woman.

"I saw something," Jem said. "A shadow." Had they scared the obia away? Why hadn't his beads protected him?

16

The hair on his arms prickled. Perhaps they had. Without them, he might be dead.

"We didn't see nothing," the man said. "We come to take the Spanish king up on his offer of freedom."

It was then that Jem noticed the brand on the stranger's cheek. A raised scar in the shape of an *R*. He winced. He'd seen such a mark before. This wasn't the first time the man had run.

"Well?" the man demanded.

"Give the boy a chance," the woman said. "He's had a start."

Jem rubbed his eyes. They'd scared off the creature. That must be the answer.

He cleared his throat. "Welcome to *Gracia Real de Santa Teresa de Mose*."

"Moh-zay?" the woman repeated. "What does that all mean?"

"It's a fancy name for freedom," Jem said, and beckoned them toward the fort.

――― ―――

"Fool likely cut himself running through the thicket," Phaedra said. She and Big Sunday peered at Jem's back. The heat from the cook fire made his wound feel as though it were aflame. "Stand still." She poked her horn nail through the tears in his shirt, lifting the fabric to inspect the scratches underneath.

"Owwww!" Jem cried. He clamped his mouth shut,

determined not to show weakness again, especially not in front of the strangers he'd brought from the forest.

"Tell me again what happened," Big Sunday said.

"It's like Shadrack said! There's something out there. A shadow creature that's half man, half beast—"

Phaedra cut him off. "Don't waste your breath asking the fool questions, Sunday. All you'll get is nonsense stories." She shoved Jem toward the chosa. "Fetch my medicine basket."

Jem got the basket and returned to the fire. Why'd she have to shame him in front of the new family? He'd near been killed by the obia, or whatever it was, and no one seemed the least bit bothered.

Phaedra and Tildy, the blacksmith's wife, had treated the new arrivals' insect bites, cuts, and blisters and ladled out bowls of stew for them. The couple ate silently, the baby asleep in her mother's arms.

"I'll see to the boy," Phaedra told Tildy. "Lean over," she ordered him. He clenched his teeth, an uneasy flutter in his belly. She slapped a poultice onto his back. It felt as though she'd jabbed the horn nail into his wounds, but he managed not to wince.

"I need a drink of water," he gasped. Biting his lip so hard he tasted blood, Jem ran to the well, where it took three buckets of water to ease the sting of her medicine. Phaedra had added salt to the usual foul-smelling mixture; he was sure of it.

But he wouldn't let her see she'd hurt him. He wouldn't have returned to the fire at all, but his curiosity about the new arrivals won out over shame and pain.

He slipped back into the group silently, careful to stand with his back away from the flames.

Big Sunday sat down across from the new couple. "Where'd you run from?" he asked.

"Up Charles Town way," the man said.

Jem looked up at the mention of Charles Town. *Had he heard of Aunt Winnie?*

"Some of us came from there. Whereabouts?"

"On Stono River. A small place...nowhere you would've heard of." The man looked at the ground.

"Rice plantation?"

"That's right," he said.

"Who was your master?"

"Died a while back. You'd not have heard the name." He glanced from Big Sunday to his wife and baby. "What's this about an oath we have to take?"

Big Sunday leaned forward. "Tell me your names again?"

The couple's eyes met and held for just a moment. "I'm Juba," the man said. "My wife's name is Adine. We've decided to call our daughter Maria."

"Fine African names," Big Sunday said. "A Spanish name for the baby?"

"Seems fitting, don't it?" Juba asked.

"Yes. Many here take new names," Big Sunday said. "But what were your slavery names?"

Juba sat straighter. "When we ran, we promised never to speak them again. They've no meaning now, and no power over us anymore."

"But what if someone in your family sends word or

wants to find you?" Big Sunday asked. "Have you thought of that?"

Adine pierced her husband with a look Jem couldn't read, and Juba stuttered, "We...we've no one to claim as kindred."

"Leave off," Phaedra told Big Sunday. "Can't you see they're afeard someone's gonna come looking?"

Juba turned toward Phaedra and started to speak, but his eyes stopped on the medallion around her neck. He stared at it until she took notice and tucked it back under her collar.

"It's a wonder you didn't change your name," Tildy said to Phaedra.

Phaedra snorted. "Well, now you know why. It's so any-one who wants to come looking can find me straightaway."

Big Sunday's mouth set in a line. He regarded the couple for a long moment. Jem didn't understand. Big Sunday had said himself that many of the maroons changed their names when they reached freedom. Why should he care what they'd been called before? He didn't suspect them of being spies for the English, did he? A couple with a little baby?

And Phaedra could talk sass all she wanted. Everyone in Mose knew she was this-county-born and didn't have an African name. Though when he studied the matter, Jem thought it odd that Phaedra hadn't just made up a new name for herself. She clearly believed she was better than the rest of them. It was a wonder she didn't have them all calling her Queenie or Majesty or some such. And what difference would it make? No one in his right mind would ever come looking for Phaedra.

Aunt Winnie had said she'd come for him. But would she? His chest pounded. What about the shadow creature in the woods? Was there an obia lurking out there in the darkness, looking for him?

He gazed toward the western wall of the fort. If something was out there waiting, Jem would be ready. He reached for his knife.

But it wasn't there. He checked the ground around him. Nothing. The last time he remembered holding it was in the woods before he'd been struck.

He must have dropped it when he fell. Or maybe his attacker took it. Between the aching in his head and the pain in his back, he couldn't think clearly. Jem closed his eyes and tried to steady his breath.

When he opened them, Big Sunday's gaze still rested uneasily on the new couple.

Jem turned to the wall and the darkness beyond.

He'd have to go back into the woods.

Chapter Three

October 14, 1739

Jem was almost glad of the many chores he needed to do. They'd give him time to think. He ran his fingers over the beads, trying to come up with a plan to slip back into the forest and look for his knife.

Already he'd fetched water, gathered eggs, and shoveled the ashes from last night's fire into the pit where they'd be mixed with lime to fertilize the fields. Now he paused while sweeping the yard and peered at the chicken scratchings on the ground. He studied the scraped earth just as Aunt Winnie had done so many times. The early morning light revealed one jagged line with a clear hatch mark through it. That could signify a boundary crossed. But what boundary? And where? And how could that help him find his knife?

If only he knew more. He had thought there'd be plenty of time to learn Aunt Winnie's teachings. She'd always been there, salving his welts and burns, setting his broken bones, even sending breath down his windpipe after Master's sons had shut him in the smokehouse.

And there were the stories. When he was hurting, sorrowful, or couldn't sleep, Aunt Winnie would tell him a story to take his mind off his troubles. As he got older, Jem noticed that the tale she chose often related to the problem he'd been worrying about. By the time he was twelve, he could usually cipher the meaning behind the story. Except for the last one. The one she told him before he left Charles Town.

It was the story of Brother Rabbit's quest. But what was its message? He thought of the ending and shuddered. *Take care when you wander into the forest.*

"You gonna sweep that dirt, or eat it?"

Phaedra's voice gave Jem such a start that he dropped the palm leaf broom. He picked it back up and began sweeping again, brushing away any signs that might have been there.

"When you're done here, rake out the chicken coop and then fetch more grass," Phaedra snapped.

Jem started to point to the drying platform, heavy with strands already turned from green to brown, but let his arm drop. Maybe the chicken scratchings had been a favorable sign after all.

Phaedra had just given him the excuse he needed to leave the fort.

⟞ ⟝

At the tree line, he hesitated, rubbing his sore back and shoulder.

The forest was a maze of light and shadow. The damp, earthy smell of moss summoned memories of the night

23

before. What if the creature still lurked nearby? He shrugged off the thought. Obias didn't come out in daytime.

Leaves rustled. He took a step backward.

For the tenth time, he searched his memory for the moment when the comforting heft of the knife's handle slipped from his grasp. Nothing.

That's when he heard the screams.

His mouth went dry, but he ran forward, through the stand of palmetto and sweet gum, into the pines, and deeper and deeper into the cool dark of the forest.

As he drew nearer, the cries became louder and more urgent. Jem's spine prickled.

Birds. That's what it was. And they sounded angry.

Scores of crows blackened the tree limbs in the clearing. One after another, they darted at something. *Caw! Caaw, caaw!* Their cries echoed like a hundred barking scolds. Jem fought the urge to cover his ears. He craned his neck and searched the treetops for the cause of their fury.

Then he saw the nest, high in the uppermost branches of a longleaf pine.

A single feather drifted down, twirling slowly through the air and landing in the pine needles at his feet. He bent to pick it up. It was ivory-colored and soft—definitely not a crow's.

He looked up again, and a ball of milky white feathers with two great eyes peeked over the side of the nest.

A baby bird.

The crows squawked angrily, taking turns flying over and

pecking at the chick. A large crow landed on the nest. Jem watched in horror as it snatched at the fuzzy baby, lifting it by the stub of a wing. The chick let out a pitiful squeal.

"Shoo, shoo!" Jem yelled, waving his arms.

But the crow paid him no mind. It lifted the baby bird into the air and shook it hard—then let go.

"Nooo!" Jem ran forward, reaching out with both hands.

But he was too late. The chick landed hard in a bed of needles.

The poor thing couldn't have been more than a few weeks old. Compared to its body, the feet were enormous, with four toes that formed sharp talons. Atop its head, two tufts of ivory feathers rose above the rest. An owlet!

Little fella never stood a chance. Jem's throat ached and the wounds on his back started to throb again.

The crows sailed off in a cloud of black, screeching their triumph.

Crouching to get a better look, Jem touched the chick's wing. The feathers were as light and soft as a whisper.

The owlet's eyes opened wide. Two fiery musket balls, glowing hot, glared from a face that seemed almost human.

"You're alive," Jem whispered.

The owlet got to its feet and lowered its head, buff-colored feathers bristling. It hopped a couple of times. One of its stubby wings was bent at an odd angle.

Jem gazed up at the nest, a good thirty feet above.

A lone caw in the distance helped Jem make up his mind. Even if he could get the baby back up there, where were the big owls that could protect it? The crows would just come back and finish what they'd started. He reached out. "I'll take care of you."

The owlet squeaked and nipped at his hand.

Couldn't blame the little critter for being wary. "You don't have to worry," he said. "I swear I'll protect you. And I keep my promises."

The owlet considered this for a moment, yellow eyes taking stock.

Jem moved slowly, taking off his shirt and gently wrapping it around the bird's body. The owlet struggled for a moment, then went still.

In the distance, the blare of a horn called the militia to drill. A slanting ray of sun sliced through the high branches, reflecting off a spot on one of the tree trunks across the clearing. Owlet safely tucked into the shirt, Jem walked over to investigate.

As he got closer, the breath left his chest in a rush.

There, driven deep into the rough bark of an ancient pine, was his knife.

＊ ＊

Later that evening, the people of Mose gathered around the circle. Jem held the owlet on a hickory plank, placed across his knees to protect them from its sharp talons. A whittled splint and scrap of cloth bound its injured wing. The owlet had not appreciated his doctoring at first, and Jem had the scratches to prove it. But finally the bird had seemed to accept it was for his own good.

A pot of oyster stew bubbled on the fire. Would the owlet eat oysters? Jem had tried beetles, but the little bird didn't want anything to do with them. Maybe he just wasn't hungry.

"There's your obia, old man." Phaedra pointed her horn nail at the owlet.

Shadrack squinted. "Did it hoot at you from this side or the other?" He pointed to the left and then to the right.

Jem hesitated, not sure of the answer.

"Whatever difference would that make?" Phaedra asked.

Shadrack glared at her. "The critter foretells good or bad fortune, depending on what side he hoots from."

Phaedra laughed so hard she almost dropped her basket. "I'd say the good luck side, then. He'll make for a tasty bite in tomorrow's stew."

"You can't eat him!" Jem said. "He's mine."

"When an owl hoots, that means someone's gonna die," Thomas said. "We should kill it."

"It's bad luck to kill an owl," Juba said.

"All I know is, that bird's a wild critter," Phaedra said. "He don't belong here."

"Don't you see?" Jem pleaded. "He'll die if I don't take care of him. He's my responsibility now."

"That's nature's way." Phaedra pulled a frond tight on her weaving and snapped off the end. "Look at those eyes. Yellow as fever," she said. "An owl's a nasty bird. I don't care about your superstitions but I know this: no good'll come of keeping it here."

"I do not know about that." A French trader named Reynard approached the fire.

27

"When'd you get here?" Jem always looked forward to his visits.

"Earlier today." Reynard took a seat by the fire. "Long ride over from Alachua." His buckskin breeches, the same reddish brown as his long hair, were coated in dust. A fine hat made of deer hide sat on his head.

Phaedra snorted and continued to work on her basket.

"I have always admired the owl," he went on. "Swallows his prey whole and casts out the bones later. Seems a sensible way to go about it." He winked at Jem. "Owl feathers are valuable to some of the tribes up north. We could make a trade if you keep him till he grows."

"Won't he need them to fly?" Jem wondered.

"I suppose he will. Maybe he will shed a couple for you."

Jem smiled. He admired the trader, the only one who didn't treat him like a child. Reynard lived life on his own terms, answering to no one. Coming and going as he chose, he crisscrossed the trails with his mule Celeste, stopping at villages along the way. In his worn leather pack he carried all manner of goods—gunflints, tobacco, fire steels, furs.

Reynard reached over, as if to pull something from behind Jem's ear. An arrowhead! He handed it to Jem.

"May I keep it?" Jem asked.

Reynard smiled and nodded. "Seems that more people are here tonight," he said. "Do you have new arrivals?"

"What do you care?" Phaedra asked. "Don't you have enough trade?"

Reynard laughed. "A trader can never have enough trade."

The owlet on Jem's lap raised its head, then settled back down on the plank.

"Wrong time." Domingo set a string of catfish on a rock by the fire.

"What do you mean?" Jem asked.

"Owls are born in winter."

And here it was only fall. Jem petted the soft down of the owlet's head. It squirmed and clacked its beak.

"*Yaba*," Domingo said.

"Does that mean owl in your language?" Jem asked.

Domingo's forehead wrinkled as though he searched his memory for the answer. Then he shook his head slowly. "It means 'omen.'"

Chapter Four

My name is Juan Antonio Rojas." The general stood with his hands on his hips, inspecting Juba and Adine.

They nodded mutely. The baby buried her face in her mother's shirt.

"You are here," said the general, "by the mercy of His Majesty, King Philip of Spain." He took off his tricorn hat and pulled at a shock of dark hair, which Phaedra swore he stiffened with egg white to make it stand on end.

"A bantam rooster with a sticky comb," she called him. "Our little Rooster General."

"This maroon fort," the general went on, "your refuge from bondage, is funded by His Majesty and by his hard-working, pious subjects in St. Augustine. Out of His Majesty's generosity, you shall each receive an allotment of corn, biscuits, and dried beef."

Jem's gaze fell on Big Sunday. The maroon captain's face remained neutral, but his giant hands clenched into fists.

"If you wish to reside in this earthly paradise of freedom," the general continued, "there shall be requirements made of you and certain conditions that must be met. You must accept the true faith and every able-bodied man must serve in the militia. You must swear an oath to the Spanish king."

Juba glanced sideways at his wife. Adine tightened her arms around Maria.

The general stared into Juba's eyes, "Furthermore, you must tell me, what information do you bring about our mutual enemy, the English?"

"What do you mean?" asked Juba.

Jem took a step closer so he could see the man's face. Was it the heat of the fire that caused him to sweat?

"How many troops are there in Charles Town?" General Rojas demanded.

"I...I don't know," Juba said. "We didn't come from there."

"Where did you come from? What is the name of the place?"

"South of Charles Town," Juba said. "Not even a town really, just a little village."

"Near Savannah?" The general leaned closer. "Those English dogs steal more Spanish land every day! Tell me, how many troops have they in Savannah?"

"Not Savannah," Juba said. "North of there."

General Rojas narrowed his eyes. "How do I know you're not spies?"

"I'll vouch for them," Big Sunday said.

The general opened his mouth to speak, but at that moment a hoarse scream pierced the twilight air.

Jem started to get up, then stopped. It was the owlet. What should he do? The corner of Phaedra's mouth twitched. Jem lit out across the yard toward the chicken coop.

The shriek sounded again.

He lifted the lid of the basket where he'd hidden the owlet. Accusing eyes stared up at him.

"What's the matter?" Jem reached down, but the owlet snapped at his hand. Gently, Jem turned the basket on its side. "Come on," he coaxed.

The owlet cried once more, then stumbled out, followed by a June beetle the size of Jem's thumb.

"Is that what you're carrying on about? A little beetle?" Jem had put the beetle in the basket himself, hoping the owlet would understand it was supper. "Eat it," he pleaded.

The general appeared at the side of the coop, others crowded behind him. "What is the meaning of this?"

"He's an owlet, sir," Jem said.

"An ugly bird," the general said.

The owlet's head swiveled at the sound of the general's voice. His feather horns rose and his beak opened in a hoarse wail.

The general covered his ears. "It has a voice like that of my late wife. Get rid of it immediately."

"But he can't fly yet," Jem said.

"Throw him off the watchtower and the creature will learn."

"He'll fall."

The general shrugged. "Then he shall be dinner."

There were whispers among the crowd. Food had been scarce of late. The King's ships had not arrived with the promised supplies and folks were getting worried.

"It's bad luck to kill an owl, sir," Jem said.

"You people and your superstitions." Rojas clicked his tongue. "I shall tell the priest he must visit here more often."

Phaedra stepped forward. "Let the boy keep it," she said. "If that birdlet can keep the rats off His Majesty's rations—should any ever arrive—it'll be of more use than some of the people hereabouts."

Jem gazed at her in disbelief. Had she truly spoken up for the owlet?

"Besides," she added, "he might be worth something once his feathers grow in."

—◦—

The better part of the day passed, and still the owlet wouldn't eat. Jem had tried corn mush, sweet potato, and beetles, but the owlet seemed scared and unsettled and wouldn't open his beak.

Jem remembered that when he was little and felt afraid, Aunt Winnie would tell him a story. "Have you heard about Brother Rabbit's quest?" he asked as he carried him to the bench outside the chosa.

Yellow eyes stared back at him, but the owlet didn't stir.

Satisfied that the creature was listening, Jem began the tale.

Brother Rabbit may have been small and weak, but he was clever. Still, cleverness wasn't enough for Brother Rabbit; he wanted wisdom. Figured he'd get it from the Sky God. So he went to see him.

"I can't just give you wisdom," the Sky God told him. "You've got to earn it."

Brother Rabbit scratched between his ears. "How?"

"By going into the forest to seek the impossible," the Sky God said.

Most would have given up right then and there, but Brother Rabbit was stubborn. Besides, he knew he was smarter than the other creatures. "Just tell me what you want and I'll get it."

"Three things," the Sky God said. "The rattle of the snake, the tail of the fox, and the tooth of the bear. If you bring me each of these, I shall grant you wisdom."

Jem sighed. If only he had the Sky God's wisdom. Maybe then he'd know what to feed an orphaned owlet. As if reading his thoughts, the owlet cried out again.

"What is it?" Jem asked. "What are you trying to tell me?"

The owlet blinked, opened its beak, and let out another eerie wail.

"He's hungry."

Jem whirled around. It was Domingo. How long had he been standing there?

"I know," Jem said. "But he doesn't like beetles."

"Try yolk." Domingo handed him an egg. "It's turtle."

Jem looked at it suspiciously. Was this a trick? "I'm surprised you want to help," he said. "Didn't you say an owl was a bad omen?"

Domingo shrugged. "Some omens are good. Some are bad. You will find out which when the time comes. Feed him the yolk."

It was hard to tell whether to trust Domingo, but Jem was out of notions about what baby owls would eat. There was nothing to lose, he decided, as he watched Domingo scale the wall of the fort in three easy steps and disappear over the other side.

Still, he'd have to be careful.

Chapter Five

October 16, 1739

Jem began owl training as soon he was done with his morning chores. "Omen," he said to the owlet. "I reckon your name is Omen." He set the scruffy bird on the packed dirt by the chosa door. Omen took a few awkward steps and clacked his beak.

"I don't care if his name is Philip of Bourbon, King of Spain," Phaedra said. "That critter is not staying under my roof."

"You said I should be allowed to keep him," Jem reminded her.

"I didn't say I'd provide a roof over his feathered head."

"We can't just leave him outside. You should have seen the way those mean old crows attacked him."

"Maybe they was aiming to have one less owl to hunt down them and theirs. I don't blame them. That critter is a vicious predator."

Jem shook his head. "If you'd seen those crows attacking him, you wouldn't say that."

"It's nature's way; when the weak join together they become strong. No telling how many crows this owlet's kin ate," she said. "Mayhap, they wanted revenge."

"He can't even fly!"

Phaedra regarded Omen with an appraising stare. As if sensing her scrutiny, the owlet puffed his downy feathers and raised his wings.

"*Puedo acariciar a tu pollo?*" Maribel asked.

Jem picked Omen up, careful of his talons. "He's not a chicken," he told the general's daughter, "and you shouldn't pet him."

"*Por favor?* I just want to feel feathers." Her strained English and squeaky voice grated on his nerves. "If you no let me, I tell my papa."

"All right, then," Jem said, deciding he'd best stay on the general's good side, especially if he wanted a place in the militia. "Just once. But be careful."

The bell at the gate sounded, and Maribel disappeared into the shade under the frame where Phaedra's grass was set out to dry.

"I have brought you a piece of lace from St. Augustine, Madame," Reynard announced as he strode into the yard.

Phaedra scowled at him and took the lace. "Is this the best you have?"

"Why, Madame," Reynard said. "The Spanish ladies are not as skilled at lace making as you are at basketry. But I assure you, this lace is the best to be had."

As Phaedra leaned forward to hand it back, the chain around her neck broke and her medallion fell to the ground.

Reynard picked it up, squinting at the etched surface. The silver glinted in the sunlight.

She grabbed it from him and shoved it into her pocket.

"A fine pendant," he said, opening his palms as if to show he meant no offense. "Unusual, too. Where did you get it?"

"It was a gift," she said.

"Someone in Charles Town?"

Phaedra glared at him. "What business is it of yours? Are you in trade with the English these days?"

He laughed. "Madame knows I am of French ancestry. I cannot abide the English any more than you can. And you're correct, it is none of my affair. It's just that in all my travels, I've never seen one like it."

"It's not for sale," Phaedra snapped. She thrust a covered basket at him. "Here's your payment."

Reynard took the basket and bowed to her before turning to Jem. "When the owlet's feathers are fully grown, we might be able to arrange a trade."

Jem watched Omen stagger in a circle around the yard. "I think he'll need them all."

Reynard smiled. "Perhaps you have something else to trade?"

"What about this whistle?" Jem pulled his latest carving from his pocket and handed it to Reynard.

Phaedra cackled. "That sorry thing wouldn't scare a chicken."

Reynard inspected the whistle, turning it over in his hands. "*Mon Dieu,*" he said. "This is fine work. I can tell you know what you are about with a knife."

Jem flushed and fought the urge to stick his tongue out at Phaedra.

"Mind, there's not a grand demand for whistles."

Jem's smile faltered.

"Still, this is such a fine one," the trader continued, "I do believe I'll offer a trade." He dug into his pack, retrieving a rolled piece of hide. "I saw you admiring my hat. You could fashion one for yourself out of this."

Jem took the hide. "I'll carve more whistles," he said. "For when you come back this way."

"*Bon*," Reynard said as he closed his pack. "Good."

"When will that be?" Jem asked.

"I do not know. Men are saying that there is trouble up north. That is what I wanted to ask your new arrivals about."

"They don't know anything," Phaedra barked. "What have you heard?"

"Just whispers." Reynard smiled, tipped his cap, and headed toward the gate.

Phaedra stared after him, rubbing her medallion. "I don't like that man."

"If you dislike him so much, why do you trade with him?" Jem asked. "You could've swapped directly with one of the Spanish ladies and had more lace."

"Mind your own business!" She inspected the lace against the light of the afternoon sun before folding and tucking it into her pocket. "And don't let me catch you gossiping with the likes of him."

"*Perdón*, Señorita Phaedra. I can teach you." Maribel emerged from under the canopy of drying grass.

"What could you possibly teach me?" Phaedra returned to her weaving.

Jem could tell when Phaedra was out-of-sorts by the vigor with which she attacked the rows of sweetgrass. From the speed of her hands, she must be powerful upset. Did she think the trader got the better of her?

"I show you how to make lace," Maribel said. "And you teach me to make baskets."

Phaedra frowned. "Keep to your lace and be grateful you have a skill. As you can see, this bothersome boy has none."

Before Jem could reply, a large hawk dove into the yard. "Omen!" he cried. Maribel screamed.

The hawk wheeled, seeming to pause in midair. Jem was too far away to help Omen, just like in the forest. The hawk landed on the roof of the chosa, surveying the owlet with cold black eyes.

Jem tried to get to him, but Omen was already limping toward the rack, dragging his injured wing.

The hawk dove again.

At that moment, Omen began to flap both his wings. He rose a few inches off the ground, propelling himself under the rack, where the drying grass shielded him.

The hawk disappeared over the eastern wall of the fort.

Omen hissed and clacked from under the canopy, tufted horns high as he beat his wings vigorously. He hadn't been injured at all! It must have been some kind of a trick.

"Clever owlet," Jem said with pride. "Did you see what he did?"

"Critter's smarter than some folks around here." Phaedra pointed the horn nail at Jem. "If you was an owlet, you would've been that hawk's supper."

Jem glared at her.

"My mama teach me before she die," Maribel said.

"Teach you what?"

"To make lace."

"I never had a mama to teach me," Phaedra snapped. "Got sold away when I was a baby."

Maribel's bottom lip quivered and she blinked hard. She backed away a few steps, then turned and ran.

Jem shook his head. Why did Phaedra have to be so hateful?

Chapter Six

October 17, 1739

Jem followed Phaedra and Big Sunday through the gate of the fort. The marching feet of the militia, which had already started toward St. Augustine, had stirred up a cloud of dust. Overhead, a flock of geese passed, forming an arrow pointed south.

"I should have brought Omen." Worry about the owlet had eaten away at Jem's excitement.

"This is an important day for Juba and Adine," Big Sunday said. "Not a time for spectacles. You were invited because you found them."

Phaedra made a clucking noise. "More like *they* found *him*. Had to pick him up off the ground."

Jem's spine tingled. He'd tried to keep from thinking about the creature in the forest.

"The boy brought them to us," Big Sunday said. "He should be witness to their oath."

"That may be, but I don't see why I need to go." Phaedra

dropped back to walk with them. Jem noticed she was wearing her good shawl. "The priests smell of garlic. Makes me sickly."

Jem looked out over the rows of drying corn, toward the trail to Apalachee. He searched for a sign of Reynard. What he wouldn't do to be truly free like the trader. Jem adjusted the cap he'd fashioned from Reynard's deerskin.

He watched a plume of white smoke rise from the forest. Shadrack was burning a load of charcoal.

Phaedra sniffed the air. "Wish Shadrack would come along with his smelly conjure bag. That'd make the priests hurry."

"It's a mercy Shadrack doesn't like town," Big Sunday said. "He scares the womenfolk. And his talk of obia would rile the priests."

"Why?" Jem asked. "Obia's just like the demons and heretics the priest told us to be on the lookout for."

Phaedra fixed him with a glare. "Keep your notions to yourself." She turned back to Big Sunday. "Shadrack's not right in the head."

"That may be," Big Sunday said. "But he knows what he's about when it comes to tending the kiln. The militia depends on him; our blades can't be forged without the charcoal he makes."

The trail rose and the Indian village came into view. The chosas were the same as those at Mose, though the tighter weave of the palms showed they were made by more practiced hands. Three women worked in a small garden, turning the soil with hoes fashioned from long sticks and whelk shells.

"Is Domingo coming?" Jem asked.

Big Sunday shook his head. "It's not expected of him."

"Doesn't he want to?" Jem asked.

"Not likely. Domingo doesn't favor crowds."

"Is that why he isn't in the militia?"

Big Sunday didn't answer at first. "Domingo was born into his mother's clan. He belongs to the village, not to Mose. Domingo's uncles were the ones who taught him to hunt and fish."

"Didn't you want to do it? You're his father." Jem would have swallowed the words back if he could, pained as they made Big Sunday look.

"It's the way it is," he said. "Always has been."

Jem was glad to change the subject. "How long has the village been here?"

"Hundreds of years, maybe more," Big Sunday said.

"Doesn't look old."

"What you see isn't old. My wife's people live close to the land, following the seasons. Before the Spanish came and disrupted their way of life, they'd pack up and move inland to live in the forest during the winter, then come back here every spring. Doesn't take long to build a chosa hut. And there's plenty of palms, grass, and shell hereabouts."

"Don't any of them want a big house?" Jem asked. "Like the ones in St. Augustine or Charles Town?"

"A wooden house? Half eaten up by bugs and rot soon as it's finished? No, I don't believe so. And the Spanish may live in fancy houses now, but when they first came, they lived here. My wife's ancestors took them in and helped them build St. Augustine."

They passed an older woman grinding corn in a hollowed-out tree stump with a long wooden pestle.

"Do the people of the village get a share of corn, beef, and biscuits from the king like we do?"

"Don't need it," Big Sunday said. "They've been living off the land and sea for as far back as time goes. One of Domingo's ancestors ruled the village when the Spanish faced starvation over a hundred years ago. If she hadn't shared her people's corn, there'd be no St. Augustine today. Now that's a story you won't hear in St. Augustine."

Jem thought about this. Did Domingo ever regret that his kin helped the Spanish? "Did you live here when Domingo was born?" he asked.

"Yes. But back when I first got to Florida, I lived in St. Augustine."

"What happened?"

"I met my wife." He pointed down a narrow path. "I worked in St. Augustine, but lived just over there," he said. "We were thinking about heading west before she took ill. Never got a chance. New folks kept arriving from the north. They needed me, so I moved back to town to lead the militia. That was five years ago."

"Domingo didn't come with you?"

"He was already your age by then. He decided to stay with his mother's people." Big Sunday's expression was strained, as though he were back there in the long ago.

You hear that, Phaedra? Jem wanted to shout. *He was my age and got to choose for himself.*

But why would Domingo make such a choice? he wondered. As if she could read his mind, Phaedra narrowed her eyes at him, a clear sign there'd be trouble if he asked any more questions.

The walls of the Castillo rose to the east as they continued toward the city gate. Jem gazed longingly at the diamond-shaped bastions. He could barely make out the outline of cannons on the gun deck. What he wouldn't give to light the powder that would launch a heavy lead ball into the belly of an English ship! If only he were allowed to join the militia.

He kicked at a pebble on the side of the road but missed, making the cloud of dust around them even bigger. Phaedra slapped the back of his neck. "Take that hide off your fool head," she ordered. "You look like that dirty trader."

Jem started to protest, but decided the better of it. He folded the cap and put it in his pocket.

Phaedra looked him over, then licked a finger and rubbed at a place on his forehead. Jem recoiled from the spit bath. If she disliked the Spanish so much, why'd she take such care about how he looked? Or how *she* looked, for that matter? But he forgot his irritation as the guards waved them through the gate.

The street they entered was narrow, lined with houses and courtyard walls. Unlike the round chosas of Mose and the Indian village, the Spanish houses were rectangular; some were two stories tall. Most were built of tabby or weathered wood, crumbling at the corners. A few were con-

46

structed from the same coarse stone as the Castillo. Wooden gratings covered the windows and balconies hung over the street, airing clothing and linens that cast shadows onto the packed dirt.

A breeze from the south swept through the street, making the clothes flutter.

Phaedra was right. St. Augustine smelled of garlic.

Chapter Seven

October 17, 1739

The plaza at the center of St. Augustine swirled with color and movement. Spanish ladies in lace mantillas shopped at market stalls stocked with jars of olives, pots of honey, and casks of wine. Children chased each other past soldiers standing at attention in heavy blue uniforms and pointed metal helmets. Jem gazed longingly at them and stood a bit straighter as he passed their ranks.

The bell tolled again. He followed Phaedra to the front of the plaza, where an altar had been set up. The tall paneled doors of the church swung open and a line of priests in black robes emerged. As they circled to inspect Adine and Juba, Jem couldn't help thinking of the crows flying at Omen. He shivered at the memory.

A priest tried to take Maria from Adine's arms, and Jem saw the whites of her eyes.

Phaedra pushed between them. "I'll hold the baby."

Adine handed her the child with a look of relief.

"Mark how those ladies look at us," Phaedra muttered. "Like we might breathe a pox on them, or slit their throats." She bobbed forward and a couple of the Spanish women drew back in surprise. Phaedra smiled innocently.

"They were probably just wanting to buy one of your baskets," Jem said.

"I ain't selling baskets today." Phaedra poked him in the shoulder. "So hush."

A horn blasted and everyone hurried to the government house.

Resplendent in a blue jacket decorated with gold buttons and silk-tasseled epaulets, the governor stepped onto a balcony overlooking the plaza. A row of soldiers faced the crowd. Big Sunday and some of the Mose militia stood at attention, looking stronger and taller than the rest. What Jem wouldn't do to be one of them!

"Welcome," the governor announced in English, "to the latest travelers to have followed His Majesty's beacon of freedom to these shores. May you bask in the glow of the true faith."

He switched to Spanish, droning on as the sun rose higher and higher. Flagstones at the back of the plaza wavered like they were underwater.

Bored, Jem looked at his hands. His fingers were black with remnants of last night's fire. He took his knife out and scraped at the ash under his nails.

When he looked up again, he saw a strange orb of light moving overhead. It took him a moment to realize it was a reflection off his knife. He tilted it, and the orb darted across the balcony onto the governor's chest. He adjusted his blade again and the light made small circles. The reflection looked like a bee flying around the governor's head. Or—Jem moved the orb slightly higher—a halo.

He glanced to each side, but everyone was focused on the balcony. Around and around he spun the light. There was a giggle nearby. Someone else coughed.

A Spanish soldier grabbed his wrist. Jem gasped and his knife clattered to the flagstones.

The soldier gave him a warning shake of the head and moved away. Jem picked up the knife and tucked it into his trousers.

The governor smiled and bowed before retreating back into the building to a chorus of applause.

A priest stepped forward and took over, his voice carrying across the plaza. "Do you vow to spill your last drop of blood in defense of the Great Crown of Spain and the Holy Faith?" he demanded.

Juba and Adine seemed startled. The priest waited. They nodded in unison. Their lips moved, but Jem could only hear Juba say, "I do."

The priest's mention of drops of blood reminded Jem of the story of Moses parting the Red Sea. As soon as he and his people crossed, the water rushed back and washed away the soldiers who would have taken them back to slavery.

"Do you swear to be the most cruel enemies of the English?" the priest asked.

"I do!"

The plaza fell silent. A tingling crept up Jem's spine; his neck grew warm. He opened his eyes, hoping his voice had only sounded loud in his own ears. But everyone was staring at him. Phaedra glared. A Spanish soldier snickered. Jem fought the urge to pull his shirt up around his burning ears. He set his gaze on a piece of oyster shell ground into the earth at his feet.

The priest cleared his throat and repeated the question. "Do you swear to be the most cruel enemies of the English?"

Juba supported Adine, who was gazing at her baby in Phaedra's arms.

And when they answered, "We do," this time it was Adine's voice he heard.

Chapter Eight

October 19, 1739

Jem pierced the yolk with the sharp point of a marsh reed.

"What in creation is that?" Phaedra asked.

"I use it to feed Omen. The yolk fills this part and drips into his mouth. See, it's hollow."

"All I see is that you're gonna ruin that bird."

"What you do mean?"

"You're gonna turn that owlet into a worthless pet. If he can't hunt for his own food, how will he survive?"

"He's too young to hunt," Jem said.

"Ain't natural! Bird was born to eat live critters, not suck yolk from a straw."

"It's just until he gets big enough," Jem said.

"Big enough for what? To fend for himself? Why'd he want to hunt when he's got you to feed him? And even if he did want to hunt, there's no owl mama to teach him how."

"I'll teach him," Jem said.

Phaedra snorted. "Well now," she said, "that is something I would sore like to see."

Jem vowed he would show her. He'd prove he could do more than sweep ashes and gather sweetgrass. He'd promised to look after Omen and Jem kept his promises.

⚊ ⚊

When Jem returned from his third trip to the well later that afternoon, he was surprised to see Phaedra in the yard. The militia was drilling and most of the other Mose residents were in the fields gathering dried corn. She must have come back to fetch her hat.

General Rojas rounded the corner of the church, his dark hair sticking straight up in the air and his gait determined.

Now she's gonna get it, Jem thought, ducking behind one of the pine trunks that held up the watchtower. Phaedra had sassed the general during his speech, made his little girl cry, and scared the Spanish ladies at the oath ceremony.

But why was he smiling?

Phaedra was tucking a stray palm frond into the brim of the hat and must not have seen him approach. She jumped when he tapped her on the shoulder.

"What is it?" She stood and faced him defiantly.

The general cleared his throat.

This was not going at all as Jem had imagined. *Go ahead and give her a piece of your mind,* he silently prompted, *before she has a chance to start in at you.*

"There are times...," the general began.

53

Here it comes. Jem leaned forward.

"There are times when a man finds himself in need of…"

"In need of what?" Phaedra said. "I thought His Majesty provided for all your needs."

The general laughed. "It is true," he said, "I have come up very far in the world as a trusted advisor to His Majesty." He must have seen the skepticism on Phaedra's face. "In His Majesty's service," he corrected. "I have advanced through the ranks and now earn a good pay." He hesitated for a moment. "My prospects are good."

"What does this have to do with me?" Phaedra asked.

"Ah, you see, I am getting to that part," he said.

Phaedra waited, her head tilted.

"I am asking you to be…"

"To be what?" Phaedra prompted.

"To be…my…woman."

Jem nearly fell over. The general fancied Phaedra?

Phaedra stared at the ground.

"It is a very lonely place, no?" the general said. "I could give you a better life. You could be a mother to my child."

Phaedra looked stricken by the prospect. She raised a hand and waved it before her face, as though he were a foul odor she could push away. "No!"

"Pardon?" he said. "Do you know what honor I have just offered you?"

"No."

"Are you saying you refuse my offer?" His voice rose.

"That's right."

"I'll not offer again."

"I should hope not."

"You have a man here? Big Sunday, perhaps?"

"No!"

"Ahh. You like Indian men. Am I right? They're not to be trusted, you know." He grabbed her by the shoulders. "I am burning with desire for you."

She pushed him hard. "You can burn in hell for all I care. If you were afire for real, I'd not waste my spit trying to save you."

"You dare to speak to me this way? When my people have offered you freedom, protection, and the salvation of true religion?"

"I do," she said. "And I know some true religion of my own. Conjure curses that'll wither your manly parts. Your priests won't be able to protect you if you ever lay hands on me again."

The general scowled at her for a long moment. Then he turned on his heel and marched back in the direction he'd come. Phaedra gazed after him, hands clenched at her sides.

The hair on Jem's arms tingled. He'd heard of such curses. Heard tell of folks "putting a fix" on a rival or "laying a dose" on an enemy. Conjuration had two sides. It could be used to heal, but it could also do harm. It was powerful magic, and one had to stay on the right side of it. He was fair certain Phaedra was bluffing. But what if she wasn't?

Jem started at a sound behind him. It was little Maria, cooing softly in her mother's arms.

"Makes you wonder, don't it?" Adine said.

"Wonder what?" he asked.

"What could have happened to that woman to make her so brave?"

"Don't you mean peevish?"

Adine's smile was sad. "You'll understand when you get older."

Why did adults have to speak in riddles? It'd save a lot of time and vexation if they'd just come out and say plain what they meant.

Chapter Nine

October 21, 1739

The beating of the *ka* drum drew them to the circle. It seemed to Jem an ancient sound, a heartbeat connecting him and the others to some part of themselves that had been lost long ago. Like Phaedra's basket making and Aunt Winnie's conjuration, it had been passed down through generations, a link to their ancestors, still strong despite the distance in time and place. All these traditions were pieces of a heritage the maroons clung to, even as they learned Spanish ways.

A crescent moon hung low over the fort. It had been several hours since the general galloped off toward the Castillo, hair standing straighter than Jem had ever seen it.

"What's got the Rooster in such a state?" Thomas asked.

Jem said nothing. When he looked at Phaedra, her jaw was set.

"It's always something with that man," Tildy said. "He looks for anything to take offence at." Omen screeched from his perch on Phaedra's drying rack. "And speaking of offence,

I don't like having that creature here." She pointed at the owlet. "The way those yellow eyes follow us around, it feels like we're being watched over by the devil himself."

"It's not the owl's eyes I'm worried about." Big Sunday nodded toward Juba and Adine. "Something ain't right with you two," he said. "I saw it soon as you got here. Now I hear there's trouble up north and I mean to know what."

Juba sighed. "We didn't have nothing to do with it." His lips formed a tight line, and the brand on his cheek reddened. "We were already looking to run, long before we heard the whispers."

"Since we found out about the baby," Adine added.

"All right," Big Sunday said. "You didn't have anything to do with it. What happened?"

"We didn't join them," Juba said.

"They tried to get him to," Adine cut in. "Some at our place were in on it, and they wanted him to go with them."

Juba stared at the fire. "I'm not proud of it. Time was, I'd have been there with the others. But with a wife and a baby on the way, I couldn't have nothing to do with it."

"Nothing to do with what?" Big Sunday said, his voice rising.

"Things had gotten bad. Worse than when I'd tried to run before. Word was, about to get even worse. New rules. Like we couldn't grow our own food, or meet in groups. Overseers had already started smashing the drums. There were some who decided it was time to stand up. Time to fight back."

There were murmurs around the circle.

"Rebellion?" Big Sunday asked.

Juba and Adine nodded slowly, heads so close they almost touched.

The bold courage of the word made Jem's heart pound. From time to time there'd been whispers in Charles Town, but nothing had ever come of them. Not that he'd heard of, anyway. *Rebellion.* He liked the way it sounded, the way its parts separated and ended with a sound of finality. When Jem had asked Aunt Winnie what it meant, she'd washed his mouth with lye soap. "Don't ever speak that word," she'd said. "Makes white men crazy and gets our people killed."

"Heard the plan was to gather in numbers and march right on out of South Carolina and all the way to St. Augustine," Juba said.

Jem drew in a breath. Now that was brave. Standing up for freedom, facing the enemy in broad daylight instead of running under the cover of darkness.

"What happened?" Big Sunday asked.

"They crossed the Stono River," Juba said. "Busted into a store near our old place. Rebels must have known there were guns and ammunition inside. That's when it turned vicious. One of the shopkeepers put up a fight. The mob killed him and another white man."

"Some of the rebels just wanted to get out," Adine said. "March south to build a new life. Come here." She swallowed hard. "Others wanted to spill blood. To make the English pay."

"Why shouldn't they want vengeance?" Phaedra asked sharply. "Plenty of our blood been spilt!"

"Plenty!" other voices echoed.

"Hush," Big Sunday said. "Let him tell it."

Juba nodded toward Phaedra. "I'm not saying they shouldn't want revenge. I got as much reason as many." He ran his finger along the scar on his cheek. "Some carried torches. Set the buildings alight. Smoke was so thick, you couldn't hardly see."

"It was as though they wanted to punish the very earth beneath their feet," Adine said.

"How many dead?" Big Sunday asked.

Adine shuddered. "Don't know."

"We left before it was over. But there's something else," Juba looked at Adine and she nodded.

"Wasn't just men killed."

"Women, too?" Big Sunday asked.

"That's right," Juba said.

"And children." Adine's voice was barely above a whisper.

The circle went silent.

Jem tried to swallow, but his mouth had gone dry. Death, especially the death of children, was a part of rebellion he hadn't accounted for.

Whoooo. Whoo-hoooo. Omen's call broke the silence. A mournful sound, and powerful lonely. Jem could imagine how some came to suspicion it meant death. The sound was more sorrowful than anything he'd ever heard.

For once, Phaedra's hands had gone still. They clenched the half-formed basket on her lap as she gazed out into the darkness.

Adine cocked her head in the direction of their chosa. "We knew then we had to go. We might not get another chance."

"Are there others coming?" Big Sunday asked.

Juba rubbed his chin. "If they ain't here by now, they been caught."

"How would you know that?" Phaedra snapped, "Did you tell someone about them? Is that how you and your woman got out alive?"

"No!" Juba shouted. "You don't know what you're talking about!"

Big Sunday held up his hands. "Did you see anyone else on the way?"

Juba shook his head. "We didn't stop for nothing. There was no turning back once we left. If we'd been caught, they'd of said we was part of the rebellion. It's what kept us going even when we was sure we couldn't take another step."

"That and our child," Adine added.

"You should've told us about this when you first got here!" Big Sunday said.

"I'm not proud of staying silent," Juba said. "But we were afraid."

"Afraid of what?" Thomas asked.

"That the Spanish wouldn't take us in if they knew." Juba put his arm around his wife's shoulder. "Or that they'd trade us back to the English if they believed we was part of the mob that killed those white folks."

"Why would they do that?" Thomas asked. "The Spanish welcome the spilling of English blood. They're the enemy of our enemy. That's why the king offered us freedom to join them."

"Don't be a fool," Phaedra said. "You think we've joined the Spanish? They like us fine sitting up here protecting their border. But that's it. We're here. Separate. How do you expect they'll feel when they hear about the killing of white women and children? White's white." She turned to Big Sunday. "They shouldn't have come here," she said, pointing at the couple. "Should have gone up into the Dismal. They've put us all in danger."

"She's the one's put everyone in danger, not us!" Adine stood and pointed back at Phaedra.

"What do you mean?" Big Sunday asked.

Jem held his breath, waiting for Adine to tell everyone what happened between Phaedra and the general.

But Juba touched her hand and Adine faltered. "Nothing."

"Sit down," Big Sunday said. "Last thing we need is to start fighting amongst ourselves. If there's trouble coming, we must face it together."

If he were going to ask, now was the time. Jem cleared his throat, hoping his voice wouldn't fail. "You ever hear tell of a healer by the name of Aunt Winnie?"

"Healer?" Phaedra's voice was shrill. "Is that what you call that old woman?"

Jem ignored her and focused on the couple.

"Can't say I have," Juba said and Adine shook her head.

"She told me she was planning to come this way."

"If she ain't here by now, I don't like her chances," Juba said.

Jem swallowed hard. He knew it was silly to worry about Aunt Winnie. She had powerful conjure magic to keep her safe. Besides, she'd sent him away. He should forget about her and focus on getting shed of Phaedra. Still, he couldn't help wondering where Aunt Winnie was, and hoping it was well away from Stono.

"There's trouble coming, all right," Phaedra said. "You can sit around this fire telling stories all you want, but it ain't gonna keep the English away." She gathered up her basket makings and left the circle.

The drummer resumed his beat, only this time it sounded like the rumble of a thousand angry feet.

Jem weighed the words in his mind. What would come of the blood spilled at Stono?

He ran his fingers over the beads again. They felt small and cold.

Chapter Ten

October 24, 1739

For the next three days, Jem searched for signs of what was to come. But the portents were scattered and confusing. An *S*-shaped line in the dirt, like the trail of a snake, meant a stranger coming. A buzzard circling the cornfield was a sign of being watched over. The cry of the old rooster wandering into the chosa foretold sorrow.

On the third day, news of the rebellion reached the Spanish.

Jem was feeding Omen a chameleon when he heard a shout at the gate.

Rojas charged into the yard, his horse nearly knocking Jem over. Omen screeched in protest, but the general didn't seem to notice. "Ring the bell!" he shouted.

Jem rushed to it. Finally, he had something worthwhile to do!

He pulled the rope until his arms were sore.

Thomas tapped him on the shoulder. "Everyone's here."

Jem took his place with the others in the shade of the watchtower.

The general paced back and forth for a moment before he spoke. "It has come to the governor's attention," he announced, "that a rebellion has taken place in the north. We have reason to believe that the English, filthy dogs that they are, will try to take revenge on the Spanish king, insomuch as His Majesty has offered sanctuary to your people."

"The militia is ready," Big Sunday said.

"Be that as it may, the governor of St. Augustine would have it known that he cannot condone the bloodshed of women and children, whom the English claim were slaughtered by the rebels."

"Is the governor aware of similar atrocities committed by the English?" Big Sunday's even tone held a hint of warning.

Rojas took a step back. "Of course. It is part of the reason our king has offered asylum. Still…"

"The people of Mose have no such blood on their hands." Jem marveled at Big Sunday's ability to match the general's formal way of speaking.

"The English have let it be known that they will track down the rebels at all cost." The general took a deep breath and puffed out his chest. "They have offered a hefty purse on the head—"

"Curse on the dead?" Shadrack broke in, scratching the base of his scalp. "Not enough to curse the living, now they curse our dead?"

"*Purse* on the *head*, you deaf fool!" Phaedra shouted.

"Not news to me," Shadrack said loudly. "We've had a purse on our heads, all of us, for years now."

"Silence!" The general glared at Shadrack. "As I was saying, our spies tell us the English have offered a reward for any escaped rebel who is returned to Charles Town."

Jem sensed movement beside him. But when he glanced over at her, Phaedra stood completely still, her back straight. It was only when he looked down at her hands that he understood the force of her anger. The strand of sweetgrass she gripped was twisted and frayed. Broken pieces littered the ground at her feet.

"The governor asks—nay demands—that any rebel arriving in St. Augustine be brought to him immediately."

"For what reason?" Big Sunday asked. "Are we to understand that the governor intends to collect the bounty?"

The general scowled at him. "Don't be absurd. The governor would merely like to hear details of the rebellion. Would you begrudge him this?"

"Do we have the governor's promise that no harm will come to any rebels who make it through?" Big Sunday asked.

"Harm? I am surprised you would even suggest such a thing."

"I have your word?" Big Sunday insisted.

Rojas squared his shoulders. "Of course."

Jem searched the crowd for Juba and Adine. Would they be considered rebels even though they'd had nothing to do with what happened up north? They'd already taken the oath, and that must count for something. It was more than

Jem had done. But did the general suspect they'd played a part in the uprising?

Jem spotted them standing near the back of the crowd. Close together, as though propping each other up, they kept the baby between them, their eyes trained on the ground. In the harsh daylight, the *R* on Juba's cheek looked raw and red, as though it were fresh.

"Is there anything else?" Big Sunday asked.

"The militia will double its drilling and will post additional watch over the fort, starting immediately," the general said.

"What about the corn crop?" Big Sunday asked. "It's ready for harvest and we'll need it come winter."

The general waved a hand in dismissal. "Let the women and children collect it. The militia will muster straightaway, in the north field," he said as he strutted toward the gates. Then he turned back. "One thing more. The English are looking for a man who is missing his little fingers."

Beside him, Jem heard a sharp intake of breath.

Rojas squinted into the crowd. "Has anyone seen such a man?"

Silence.

Omen screeched. He'd fallen from his perch and was now hanging by his feet, toes clutching the branch that hung near Phaedra's stand. His wings flapped furiously but ineffectively. Jem rushed over to him.

The crowd began to disperse. Phaedra came over and stood beside Jem. She stared at a patch of whitewash and a pellet on the ground beneath the stand.

"I'll sweep it away," he promised her.

"Find that creature another roost," she said. "I don't like the way he's been looking at the chickens."

"He's no threat to the chickens," Jem said. Adult feathers had begun to replace Omen's soft, pale down. Weaned off egg yolk, he'd finally started eating beetles, crickets, and small lizards. But nothing larger.

"That may be the case now, but soon he will be. And I don't like to hear them squawking when he gets near."

"I'll make a new perch for him."

Jem glanced at her out of the corner of his eye. She stood motionless, gazing at the flock spread out along the north wall.

"We're just like those chickens," she said, "set out here in this oversized coop to squawk a warning when the English come. Mark my words. When they do, there's gonna be a slaughter."

Chapter Eleven

October 26, 1739

S*queee, squeee, squeee.* Omen's beak stretched wide. Jem had learned this meant the owlet was hungry. He wasn't the only one. It had only been two days since the militia doubled its drilling and increased the watch, but already there was more water and fewer fish in the noontime stew. Jem and the others sat on the benches arranged around a small cook fire.

Five days had passed since they learned of the rebellion and he was no closer to breaking free of Phaedra. If he didn't do something to prove he belonged in the militia soon, it'd be too late to catch up with the others. A blue heron passed overhead, a small mullet in its beak. That gave Jem an idea. "I could catch us some fish."

Phaedra snorted. "You couldn't catch a starfish."

But Big Sunday had overheard. "It's about time the boy learned."

"You'll teach me?" Jem asked.

Big Sunday shook his head. "None of us in the militia can spare the time to catch fish, much less teach someone else how."

Jem's shoulders fell. Desperate, he came up with another idea. "What about Domingo?"

Big Sunday pursed his lips. "I don't know," he said. "You'd have to talk to him."

Jem started to protest, then nodded. Why was it that Phaedra, who wasn't even his kin, could order Jem around all day and night, while Big Sunday wouldn't even ask his own son to take Jem fishing? "I'll find him first thing tomorrow," he said.

"That's all well and good, but there's a chore needs doing here first," said Phaedra. "The fort needs a new privy hole. You'd better start digging now, so you'll be done before tomorrow."

⁓ ⁓

Jem shoveled another bit of dirt out of the shallow pit. It was just past noon, and he hadn't dug but a few feet into the sandy soil near the northwest wall of Mose.

At the rate he was going, finishing the privy hole would take all day.

That was fine with him.

In fact, he'd see that it did. He couldn't go to the village to find Domingo until tomorrow, and he didn't want to take the chance that Phaedra would invent new tasks for him.

"Should of known you couldn't be trusted to dig a simple

hole," Phaedra said when she came to check on his progress.

"Lot of rocks and roots hereabouts," Jem replied, his shovel hitting an imaginary barrier.

"I don't see any."

"They're hard to see, but they go deep. Can't always get them dislodged."

"Expect not. Especially when you're a wee little runt with no muscle."

Jem wouldn't fall into her trap. "Expect not," he repeated, and kept trying to push his shovel around an imaginary rock.

When he glanced up again, she was gone.

Jem smiled and worked for another half hour without moving more than a few shovels of soil.

"What is the meaning of this?" The general's shiny brown boots appeared at the edge of the pit.

"Digging a new privy hole, sir."

"On whose orders?"

"Phaedra's."

"Why wasn't I made aware that a new privy was needed?" he asked.

"That's Phaedra for you, sir," Jem said. "She does as she pleases and doesn't care overmuch for following orders." He let his reply sit for a moment, then added. "You're well rid of her, General. And it's my personal opinion she has no knowledge of conjure curses such as she threatened you with, so you can rest easy on that count."

Rojas glared at Jem, nostrils wide, eyes narrow. "I have no idea what you're talking about."

"You know, when she said she'd—" Jem could see by the general's expression that he'd made a mistake. He picked up his shovel and started digging furiously. The general stood there a few moments, then stalked off.

Late in the afternoon, Tildy hollered like she'd stumbled into a dagger plant. "There was three of them!" she yelled. "Three fat mackerel. Right here!" She pointed to the smoking rack.

A crowd had gathered and everyone looked at Jem.

"I didn't take them," he said. "Been digging all the day long."

"Not *you*," Tildy said. "*That* creature took them." She pointed to Omen, sitting on the new perch Jem had made for him. The owlet swiveled his head toward the watchtower, following a sparrow in flight.

"Omen doesn't fancy fish," Jem said.

Big Sunday shook his head. "Boy...," he began.

"I know it wasn't him," Jem said. "He won't eat fish."

"What kind have you given him?"

"Crawfish I got from the creek," Jem said. "He didn't want anything to do with them."

Omen made a call that sounded like laughter. He quieted, blinked a few times, and strained his neck forward.

Jem held his breath. *Not now, please, not now!*

Omen opened his mouth wide, and out came a pellet.

Big Sunday prodded it with the toe of his boot, scattering the contents. "He may not like crawfish, but he has a taste for mackerel."

"I didn't know," was all Jem could say as he looked in amazement at the fish bones in the pellet. "But I'll catch more! I promise!"

"That owlet belongs in the forest," Big Sunday said gently. "Not here."

The wind left Jem's chest in a rush. "But I owe him," he said in a whisper, not trusting his voice. "I saved him from the crows and he's my responsibility. I can't just throw him over the wall to fend for himself. I've got to make sure he can fly. I promised."

"We can't have him eating our stores," Big Sunday said. "We need all we've got and then some."

Omen leaned forward and opened his beak again. But instead of casting more fish bones, he let out a loud and insistent wail. Jem knew the sound. It was the one the owlet made when he was hungry.

Chapter Twelve

October 26, 1739

Omen was restless. Three times he called out in the night, *who-hoo, who-hoo, who-hoo,* as though on sentry duty.

Jem wrapped a blanket around his shoulders and slipped out of the chosa. The yard was quiet and not a trace of a breeze stirred. He found the owlet stalking around the edge of the coop in the moonlight.

He tried to tempt Omen with a tree frog he'd captured in the woodpile. If only he'd had the frog earlier, maybe the owlet wouldn't have eaten the fish. Jem's temples pounded as he pondered what Big Sunday had said about letting the owl go. What if Omen stole more fish? He shook his head. He'd make sure that didn't happen. But how? Wasn't it time Omen started catching his prey? True, he couldn't yet fly, but he had to start somewhere and what could be more tempting than a plump frog?

But while the owlet watched the frog intently, his head turning almost a full rotation, he made no move to catch it as it hopped away from the coop.

"Now see here!" Jem said. "I won't go scaring up critters for you, just to have you turn your beak up at them!" Realizing his voice was too loud, he whispered, "That was a fine frog!"

Omen blinked hard, and Jem felt ashamed of himself. He couldn't blame Omen for being unsettled. The owlet was just like him, all alone.

Jem gazed up at the night sky. Miles away, a flash of heat lightning pierced the darkness. "Remember the story I told you about Brother Rabbit asking the Sky God for wisdom? Want me to tell you how he got Snake's rattle?"

Omen swiveled his head and peered at Jem as he tried to remember the exact words Aunt Winnie had used. He spoke slowly and deliberately.

Snake was a proud one. Some say he was vain. Liked to look at the pattern of his scales and admire the path he cut in the dirt. But he was especially proud of the sound his rattle made. One stormy day, Brother Rabbit found Snake in his den and said, "You got a fine rattle, Mr. Snake. Too bad it ain't loud enough to drown out the rain."

"Fool," Snake told him, "my rattle is far more powerful than the rain."

"Maybe it is," Brother Rabbit said, "but I can't hear it so well."

Snake commenced to rattling, and Brother Rabbit began backing away toward the entrance of the den.

"Rain's getting louder," Brother Rabbit said. Snake rattled harder.

Just as the storm was about to hit, Brother Rabbit hopped out of the den. Snake followed after him, shaking his rattle so hard he couldn't hear the thunder getting closer.

All of a sudden, a bolt of lightning came down and split the rattle right off Snake's tail.

As if responding to the story, Omen made the call that sounded like laughter. He stalked about, opening and closing his wings, which both seemed to work fine now.

Jem entered the fenced enclosure and arranged some fresh hay. The chickens clucked and sputtered before finally settling on their roosts.

He lay down, covered himself with his blanket, and let Omen climb onto his chest. "See?" he said, tracing a finger along the path of the stars that formed the drinking gourd. He pointed to the North Star. "It's the only one that doesn't change places." Aunt Winnie had shown it to him, telling him someday he might need to find his way at night.

Omen wouldn't be still. The heavy bird paced back and forth across his chest. When it neared his face, Jem drew the blanket up to his chin and Omen hopped off.

A few moments later, Jem was startled by a tug to his hair. "Cut that out!" he said.

Omen pecked gently at his ear. Jem giggled.

Then a noise from outside the coop made him draw in his breath.

Someone was there, moving through the yard.

Jem could barely make out a dark silhouette on the other side. *Probably just going to the privy,* he told himself. But he didn't really believe it. There was a slow stealthiness to the movements. Whoever it was didn't want to be seen.

Jem tried to nudge the owlet away so he could get a better look, but froze when Omen squawked and clacked his beak.

He sat up, his back to the rail of the coop.

The owlet made cooing sounds and rubbed his beak against Jem's palm, searching for beetles. Jem petted the soft feathers on his head. As he stared out at the sky beyond the fort walls, Jem had the peculiar sensation that someone was watching him. Omen must have sensed it, too. He turned his head in the direction of Jem's secret path over the wall. Could the owlet see what was out there in the darkness?

———

"Don't get wet," Phaedra warned him.

"I don't even know if Domingo will teach me," Jem answered. But how'd she expect him to fish without touching the water? Dread wiggled like a worm in his stomach. What if he fell in, got taken up by the current, and carried out to sea?

"And I won't have you wandering about bare like those boys over yonder," she called as he headed out the gate. Jem's cheeks burned at the indignity.

The streets were quiet in the Indian village. A couple of men sat at a cane frame, tying a fishnet. A woman stirred a pot over a low fire. Another called to a group of children playing nearby.

Jem noticed for the first time how the tall church seemed out of place next to the low round chosas. Its outline looked harsh and overbearing. It wouldn't last as long as the chosas either. The boards touching the earth were riddled with rot and insect holes.

Domingo and another boy stood at opposite ends of a split pine trunk about six feet long, set horizontally on two thick logs. A small fire burned in its center. Using straws made from marsh reed, they blew on the embers, slowly spreading the fire to both ends of the trunk.

The wind changed and a cloud of smoke blew into Jem's face. He coughed. "What are you doing?"

"Making a canoe," Domingo said.

As the flame got close to his side of the trunk, the other boy dipped some moss into water and used it to slow the fire.

Jem felt like an intruder. The older boys probably wished he would leave, but he couldn't bring himself to go. And he hadn't yet gotten up the courage to ask about fishing. Besides, he was handy at carving, and the canoe making intrigued him. "Can I try?" he finally asked.

Domingo said something in their language to his friend, who handed Jem a straw.

It wasn't hard once you got the wood burning. But it was slow and tedious work and Jem soon became bored and restless. He scanned the long expanse of untouched surface and got an idea to make the work go faster. Using their method, he burned a narrow trench along the edge of the trunk and filled it with water. Then he set a larger fire nearer the center. He wasn't worried, because if the flame got too close to the edge, the water would stop it from spreading. He'd show Domingo he was all kinds of clever and could help him get the canoe finished in no time.

Jem scraped out a longer section of the trunk so the fire would spread more easily. Next, he worked the flame over the gouged wood. He even put a little dried grass on top to help it burn. He smiled. Just as he had suspected, the flame soon spread over a large area.

And then it kept going. It leapt right over the little trench he'd dug and reached out toward the edges of the trunk.

Domingo grabbed a bucket and dumped water on the flames.

Jem glanced at him, expecting to get a scolding. But Domingo didn't appear angry. If anything, it looked as though he might laugh.

"You knew that would happen!" Jem said.

The older boy shrugged.

"Why didn't you tell me? You saw what I was about!"

"You wouldn't have believed me." Domingo smiled. "Better to learn by doing."

Chastened, Jem decided to change the subject. "Could you teach me to fish?"

Domingo looked surprised. "All right. Tomorrow."

A thought struck Jem. "Is the water deep?" he asked. "It's not that I can't swim," he added. "It's just that I'm not accustomed to the currents hereabouts." He swallowed hard.

Domingo drew an oyster shell across the area he'd burned, removing the burnt wood to reveal the strong wall of the canoe. "No need to swim," he said. "The water is not so deep."

If that was the case, why did Jem sense he was already in over his head?

Chapter Thirteen

October 28, 1739

Jem stood in creek water up to his knees. "I don't see any fish."

Domingo raised his slender spear and launched it at a spot several feet away. It shot into the water without a splash. When he drew it out, a shiny mullet was attached.

Jem searched the water around him and finally saw a fat catfish. But when he threw his spear, its point missed the target by almost a foot.

"Aim lower," Domingo said. "The light on the water makes the fish seem higher than it is."

But Jem's first attempt must have scared all the fish away. He didn't see any others. He sighed loudly.

Domingo held a finger to his lips and stood quietly. They waited for what seemed like an hour. The older boy threw his spear again and again, catching a gar, a mullet, and a flounder.

Jem grew tired of staring at the creek bottom. His spear was becoming heavy. He watched a crawfish chase a tiny crab across the sandy surface of the creek bottom.

Whoosh! Domingo added another mullet to his string.

"You should've seen the fish they have back in Charles Town," Jem said, gripping the spear under his chin and stretching both hands wide. "This big."

Domingo nodded. He was already moving up the creek, scanning the water in search of his next catch.

It was hard to stand still enough not to scare off the fish. Jem's head itched. What if he'd picked up some lice? He shuddered, hoping he was wrong. If Phaedra caught wind of it, there'd be no stopping her. She'd be all over his scalp with the horn nail and a dousing of goose grease.

"Couldn't we go somewhere else?" he asked. "Some place where the fishing is—"

Swoosh! Domingo threw his spear in one fluid movement. Another mullet. The biggest so far.

"—better?" Jem finished his sentence.

"If you want, we could go to the bay," Domingo said.

Jem liked the sound of that. Maybe he'd get to see the soldiers drilling. Maybe they'd even be practicing with the cannon. He followed Domingo back to where they'd left the canoe in the grass downstream.

After they had paddled for a short while, the creek narrowed and the marsh grass formed a thick wall that rose up on both sides of the canoe, blocking sight of the land on either side. The grass itself was divided by the tide line— somber gray blue on its lower reaches where water regularly drenched it, and vibrant yellow green above.

Jem paddled a bit faster, eager to put this section behind him and get out into the open water. He couldn't seem to get enough breath, as though the tall grass had stolen it all up.

Like in the maze in Charles Town.

When he was small, Master's sons would chase him into the back garden. There, taking up almost an acre of land, rows of bushes had been trained to grow together and trimmed to form corridors that twisted and turned to form a maze. Some led forward and others ended abruptly in a tall wall of green. There was only one way out at the other end. Sometimes, in his dreams Jem still saw the terrifying vision of the path dead-ending in front of him as the taunts of his pursuers became louder and louder.

He swallowed. "Are we gonna be out of this soon?"

Domingo dropped his paddle, picked up two cane poles from the bottom of the boat, and handed one to Jem. "Like this," he said. He used his pole to push off lightly from the muddy floor of the marsh and moved the canoe gently through the channel.

Hoping to get them out of there more quickly, Jem plunged his pole into the dark water beside the canoe and gave it a mighty shove. But the pole stuck in the mud. The canoe surged ahead, while the pole pulled Jem backward. He could either let go or fall into the water.

He let go. The pole sprung to attention, spreading a ring of ripples. He grabbed for it, but the movement made the canoe sway violently. Jem dropped to the floor to keep from falling out.

The rocking slowed and Jem looked up. Domingo stood, feet spaced apart and knees bent slightly, balancing his own pole horizontally. The canoe steadied. Jem sunk lower into the canoe, bracing for the chiding he knew was coming.

Instead, Domingo began to laugh softly. He pointed at the lost pole, standing upright in the water about ten feet back.

A tern landed on it and scolded them.

Domingo laughed even harder, so much that he shook the canoe. Jem joined in. The tern gave a final cry and flew off.

With a few light pushes, Domingo had the canoe back beside the stuck pole. He dislodged it from the mud and handed it back to Jem.

They continued west toward the Castillo. A blue heron passed low overhead, casting a shadow on their path through the tall grass. The waterway widened and they entered a bigger channel. Stowing the poles, they began to paddle again.

The rhythm was soothing and Jem was able to forget his troubles with Phaedra and his worries about Omen. He wasn't even quite as afraid of falling in the water as he'd been when they started. There was something otherworldly about the marsh that made him feel they'd crossed a boundary and entered into a place time had forgotten. A place where there were no English and no Spanish. Where anything was possible.

A hill rose abruptly from the bank to their right. "What's that?" Jem asked. "If we climbed up there, I bet we'd see clear to St. Augustine."

"Sacred place," Domingo said.

"Did someone build it?" Jem peered at the slope as they passed, but there was nothing holy looking about it. Just a mound covered with a mix of marsh grass, vine, and palmetto.

"The old ones."

"Your ancestors?" Jem asked. "Are they buried there?"

Domingo nodded. "Before the Spanish come, there are many villages, many people."

"Where'd they go?"

Domingo's shoulders tensed. "Taken. Or dead. Some are buried there."

They kept a wide path of water between them and the mound. "How'd they die?"

"Sickness brought by Spanish killed most. Also, slave traders come."

"Your people were enslaved, too?" Jem asked. "You got kin in Carolina?"

Domingo's paddle sliced through the water. "They try. But my people are of the land. The swamps, forests, and marshes are our home. Slave traders sell us north, we make our way back. It is no hardship. The English learn this and make a new plan. They send us across the sea. A far place called West Indies. None return."

Jem swallowed hard. He'd never thought about how Domingo might feel about the Spanish and English. He wanted to say something, but wasn't sure what. He bowed his head as they paddled past the mound.

A loud barking, like a pack of dogs, came from off in the distance.

Jem shuddered. In Charles Town, patrollers used dogs to search the streets after curfew. "Those dogs sound fierce."

"Not dogs."

"You sure?" Jem tried to see through the marsh grass.

"Crocodiles."

"What got them so fired up?" Jem said. "They sound mighty angry."

"Not angry. Hungry."

Jem's breath caught. "We're not headed their way, are we?"

Domingo just smiled.

"What would you do if you came across one?" Jem asked.

Domingo regarded him quizzically. "Run."

They rounded a bend, and the walls of the Castillo rose from the shallows. The air smelled of low tide, and pools in the dark sand at the shoreline twinkled with reflections of white stone. Beyond, the wharf and buildings of St. Augustine hugged the mouth of the bay. Small boats and pirogues dotted the waterfront. Gulls circled and wheeled around a fishing boat.

"How are we gonna catch anything with all these boats about?" Jem asked "Aren't there too many?"

"Big fish follow the boats," Domingo said.

"Sharks?"

Domingo shrugged and slipped from the canoe into the water.

Jem wished he'd been more patient at the creek. The water wasn't very deep here, but there was so much of it. He tried to hide his fear as he took off his shirt, rolled up his pants legs, and eased out of the canoe.

Domingo was right. The schools of fish were so thick that even with his clumsy spear throwing, Jem couldn't help but catch some. Tied to a heavy stone at the bottom of the bay, the canoe bobbed between them. The sun beat down on his back.

Fishing was easy once you got the hang of it. Wouldn't they be surprised when he came back with enough fish to feed the whole militia? That would show Phaedra.

"We should go back now," Domingo said.

"Not yet," Jem pleaded. Intent on following a school of redfish that were about to be trapped by the changing tide, he strayed farther from the canoe. If he could catch just a few more...

"Look!" Domingo called.

But Jem now had the biggest fish he'd seen all day in his sights. He waved in the direction of Domingo's voice, not wanting to make a sound. This was a fish that would prove he could do more for Mose than clean chicken coops. If he were just stealthy enough and quick enough... *Swoosh!* He let the spear fly.

"You there, boy!" a man shouted.

Jem stood rooted to the spot, staring down at the fish as it twisted and thrashed, fighting to free itself. Only the tailfin was caught. Jem envied the fish. It hadn't frozen when it was in danger.

He had. And what had paralyzed him wasn't the shout itself. It was the voice.

An English voice.

Chapter Fourteen

October 28, 1739

How had the boat gotten so close without him seeing it? Jem wondered if he should drop the spear and try to wade in. If he made it to the shallows, he could get to the shore and run back to Mose.

But his shirt was still in the canoe. And without Aunt Winnie's beads, he had no protection.

Maybe the Englishman's command wasn't directed at him. Maybe if he stayed still, they'd go away. He closed his eyes and willed himself invisible. There was a whoosh of water at his feet. He opened his eyes. The fish wiggled off his spear and brushed against his legs as it swam away, a flash of silver disappearing toward the sea.

When Jem looked up, he saw three men in a flat-bottomed boat.

"He one of yours?" the man in front said in English.

"No, but maybe he can lead me to them."

"Drop the spear!" the first man ordered.

Rough hands grabbed Jem under his arms and hauled

him up onto the deck. Two white men with tricorn hats stared down at him. The man who held him was an Indian who wore the dark tattoos of a northern tribe.

"Don't move. And don't get the cargo wet!"

Jem's stomach lurched. How could he have been so careless? What if these men took him back to Charles Town? He thought of the brand on Juba's cheek. Being marked by the skin-searing iron wasn't the worst of the punishments for running. He had to get away from them. But how?

"Where are my people?" the second man demanded. "Blacksmith and his wife. I know they're here!"

Jem tried to keep his eyes wide and vacant with the houseboy look Aunt Winnie had taught him. A plan started to form in his mind. He thought of Brother Rabbit tricking Snake into going out in the storm. "I…I could take you to them."

"Don't bother with him, Pierce," the other man said. "It's plain the child's a half-wit."

Domingo was already back in the canoe, paddling away toward the river. Jem's eyes stung, but he understood. With three men on board, what could Domingo have done? Besides, he had as much reason to fear the English as Jem did.

"Where are they?" Pierce asked again.

Jem was sure of it now. His best chance was to pretend to lead them to Mose and then break away from them somehow. He knew the forest much better than any Englishman. "Just north of here," Jem said. "I'll take you to them."

Pierce smiled. "It's just as I told you, Williams. The meddlesome Spanish lured them here with promises of freedom!"

"What now?" his friend asked.

"We're going straight to the governor. I will have satisfaction."

Jem swallowed hard. "No need for that, sir. I can show you were they are. I believe they've been waiting for you to come fetch them."

"You sure it's safe to go to the Spanish governor?" Williams asked, ignoring Jem.

"I've been doing business with him for a long time," Pierce said. "How do you think St. Augustine survives when the Spanish supply ships don't come? On English rice, that's how. The governor owes me."

Jem felt dizzy. Phaedra said the Spanish had short memories when it came to their promises. Would the governor let Pierce seize Thomas and Tildy? The boat bumped against the wharf and he nearly fell overboard.

"Move." Pierce pushed him onto the dock. "Stay here," he called over his shoulder to the Indian man, "and make sure no one touches the rice."

As he stumbled toward the plaza, Jem had the peculiar feeling of being in a dream—a nightmare where you know you should run, or at least cry out, but instead you follow along on a path your wakeful self would rebel against.

They met few people on the street. St. Augustine had retreated behind courtyard fences for the midday meal. From behind the shuttered windows, there came low voices and the clank of cutlery on plates.

"Jem! Jem!" He heard footsteps and then the governor's daughter Maribel was at his side. "What are you doing with these Englishmen?"

"Go away, little girl," Williams told her.

Maribel narrowed her eyes at him. "You are not in charge here! You must let Jem go. My father will be angry if you do not."

A shuttered window flew open and an old woman stuck her head out. "*Qué es esto?*" she demanded.

Pierce doffed his cap. "*Buenos días, Señora,*" he said.

Maribel kicked Pierce in the shin and ran. "Come on, Jem!" she cried.

But before he could take a step, a hand clamped down on his wrist. Williams had him.

Maribel headed down the street. "When my father hears," she called over her shoulder, "you will be sorry!"

They pushed Jem ahead of them. As they rounded the corner they came upon Reynard trading with a Spanish tinsmith. He tipped his cap to Pierce and Williams, taking in the scene without so much as a raised eyebrow. Jem gazed at the trader, eyes wide and teeth clenched, trying to signal he was in trouble.

"What have we here?" Reynard asked. "A mischievous boy causing trouble?"

"We found him in the harbor," Williams said. "We're sure he was up to no good."

"I can take the boy off your hands if he's bothering you," Reynard said. "Got a load of tin needs shifted and I could use some help."

"Do it yourself, trader," Pierce said. "Or get your old mule to haul it. The boy comes with us."

"Maybe I'll come along," Reynard said casually. "I have some trading to do in the plaza."

"Unless you're trading with the governor these days," Pierce said, "we're not headed in your direction."

Jem's shoulders slumped. He was stuck, caught. No one could help him now.

The guards at Government House didn't look surprised to see the Englishmen. One led them down the long hallway to the governor's chambers and left them there without a word.

"*Señor* Pierce!" the governor exclaimed. "What a lovely surprise."

Jem's stomach churned. But then he noticed that the governor had two smartly dressed soldiers stationed directly behind him.

"Governor," Pierce said. The two Englishmen bowed slightly. "I believe you know Williams."

The governor inclined his head. "You bring us more rice?"

"Yes, I've brought rice. But I have another score to settle with you first."

"If anyone has offended you," said the governor, "I shall scold them soundly. It is my wish to offer you only friendship and hospitality."

"Then you will hand over my property."

"Why, sir." The governor sounded hurt. "I have no idea of what property you speak."

The soldiers behind him shifted.

"You have two of my people here."

"You must be mistaken. We have no English in our humble town."

"Stop playing games, Governor. I'm talking about my

slaves. This one claims to know where they are." A push sent Jem stumbling forward.

The governor gazed on Jem as though he were an ant in the honey crock.

"I can explain," Jem said.

"Shut up, boy." The Englishman grabbed him again by the scruff of his neck. "I'll have my people back, if you please."

The governor narrowed his eyes. "If you are referring to the souls to whom my king has promised religious sanctuary, I'm afraid the matter is out of my hands."

"Religious sanctuary?" Pierce laughed. "Slaves have no religion. Your people stole them from me and I want them back."

"It is not possible," the governor said. "They appealed to the king and have become devout Catholics."

"Ha! This one says they don't like it here."

The governor squinted at Jem. "The boy is an idiot. Those you seek have requested sanctuary."

"Sanctuary from what?" Pierce yanked Jem's shoulder hard. "I treat my servants well. They eat better than most people in St. Augustine. Someone here lured them away."

"I must tell you again," the governor said, "I have no authority to do as you ask. I am sworn to follow the orders of my king."

"Funny how you Spanish heed some of your king's orders but ignore others. You're only too happy to buy English rice."

"If English pirates would cease their plunder of Spanish

supply ships, we'd have no need of your rice." There was a hard edge to the governor's voice.

Pierce laughed.

The governor narrowed his eyes. "And where would you be then, *Señor* Pierce? Certainly not making a profit from the hardship of my people. Let's not forget, you don't give the rice away."

"Yet it seems I've been doing just that." Pierce raised his hands in the air. "You owe me money, governor. And your credit has run out."

The men glared at each other for a long moment. Jem felt a trickle of sweat run down his back.

Pierce broke the silence. "I suppose you've heard about the rebellion up north."

"Such a shame," the governor replied.

"Does your king extend religious sanctuary to killers?"

"I don't know what you're talking about." For the first time, the governor looked uncomfortable.

"Did you know the slave rebels at Stono killed women and children?"

"We get so little information, isolated as we are—"

"I'm sure your spies have told you plenty."

The governor drew a weary breath and steepled his fingers. "I'm sorry I can't help you. Now if you'll excuse me—"

"What about this one?" Pierce had Jem again by the back of the neck.

"I am a free man," Jem said, desperate to remind the governor of his King's promise. "And a subject of His Majesty King Philip of Spain."

"Shut your mouth, boy!" The Englishman's nails bit into his skin.

Heavy footsteps sounded in the hall. Jem heard the door behind him swing open. Pierce's grip loosened.

"You brought quite a delegation," the governor said to the men in the doorway. "Am I to understand the boy is one of yours, Captain?"

"Yes, sir." It was Big Sunday's voice, deep and measured. "My son said there was trouble."

Big Sunday had come for him. And he hadn't come alone. Domingo and five of the strongest men in the Mose militia stood behind him, forming a line that blocked the door.

"There's no trouble here," the governor said. "I believe *Señor* Pierce was just leaving."

Pierce and Williams turned to go, but the line of men held fast. Pierce glared at them but their faces remained calm and expressionless. Finally, Big Sunday nodded and the men from Mose broke ranks to let them pass.

"You haven't heard the last of this," Pierce said.

"I expect not," the governor sighed.

"And don't expect any more rice."

When he'd put a bit more distance between himself and the men from Mose, Pierce spoke again, and his words echoed through the corridor. "You'd think twice about offering sanctuary if you saw what they did at Stono. Were I you, Governor, I'd sleep with one eye open."

When the sounds of their footsteps faded, the governor cleared his throat. "Captain, I'll thank you to take this boy out of my sight. His childish games have caused an unnecessary exacerbation of troubles and contributed to the severing of a trade relationship which had formerly provided necessary food supplies to St. Augustine. Pierce will be telling all of Charles Town and Savannah we're stealing their slaves. Soon none of them will sell us rice."

"But I—" Jem started.

"Yes sir," Big Sunday interrupted, silencing Jem with a heavy hand on his shoulder.

"I take it the child was lying about Pierce's former slaves wanting to return to his plantation?" asked the governor.

"I was only—" Jem started to explain, but the governor held up his hand.

"Now, Captain."

"Yes, Governor," Big Sunday said.

Why did Big Sunday look so angry? Who was he mad at? Pierce? The governor?

Or, thought Jem, *could I be the one he is angry with?*

Chapter Fifteen

November 3, 1739

A week had passed since the incident with Pierce, but still no one was speaking to Jem. When he'd tried to explain how his offer to bring Pierce to Thomas and Tildy was part of a trick, Big Sunday didn't want to hear it. Only Omen seemed to understand—to know Jem had just been trying to help. The owlet still crawled onto Jem's shoulders, took beetles from his fingers, and gazed at him with glowing eyes, even if the rest of Mose treated him as though he wasn't worthy of their company.

Omen had found a new favorite spot now that he had grown too big to lodge with the chickens. He'd learned to use his talons to climb the log posts at the base of the watchtower; now he spent most of the day and night on a crossbeam about eight feet up from the ground.

"It's downright unnatural the way he watches us." Tildy glared up at the owlet as she and Phaedra ground corn in the yard. "The creature never sleeps. Last night I got up to use the privy and nearly jumped out of my gown when I saw those yellow eyes glaring down at me."

Picturing how that might have appeared to the night watch, Jem couldn't hold back a chuckle.

Tilly and Phaedra glared at him. Then they remembered they weren't speaking to him and looked away.

"I'm just saying that it's hard for a body to rest with such in our midst," Tildy went on.

"From the snores coming from your bed, you seem to manage." Jem could tell from Phaedra's tone that her heart wasn't in the baiting.

Tildy's mouth dropped open. "I do not snore!" She stormed off in the direction of the forge.

Jem put on his buckskin sleeve, went over to the watch-tower, and called to Omen.

The owlet gazed down at him but did not move.

Phaedra spoke as though to her basket. "That fool boy made yon birdlet weak by feeding it turtle yolk and fish, just like that old woman in Charles Town made him soft."

"She did not!"

But Phaedra continued as though she hadn't heard his protest. "Sure as she filled his head with foolish notions about those silly beads. How's he ever gonna learn to be a man?"

Jem turned his back on Phaedra, but her words dug into him, sharp as Omen's talons.

He tried again. "Here, Omen."

This time the owlet hopped onto his outstretched arm and let Jem pet his head. His wings, now much longer, were covered with brown plumage. He still had the same soft ivory feathers on his legs. Strange-looking bumps had appeared underneath his toes. These little claw pads helped him grip branches, though he still had trouble staying upright. It wasn't unusual to find him hanging upside down, wings beating as he tried to right himself.

"Claimed he'd have that birdlet flying by now," Phaedra muttered. "Said he'd fly by the time the leaves changed. Guess he was just fooling himself."

Jem pretended to ignore her. But she was right.

Omen should be flying by now.

A sudden breeze stirred the limbs of a nearby maple, releasing a shower of red leaves. They spiraled and circled around Jem, blocking out the sun for a moment, before coming to rest on the packed dirt at his feet.

How could Omen survive on his own if he couldn't fly? How long would it be before someone decided he belonged in the stew pot? As Jem gazed up at the emptying branches, it seemed to him that time was running out.

～ ～

The next afternoon, Jem approached the gate carrying a big lidded basket. His plan was to say he was going out to dig roots in the forest.

But before Jem could speak, Omen objected loudly to his confinement in the basket.

"Shhh," Jem whispered.

"What you got there?" Juba asked from the sentry post.

"J...just a basket. Figured I'd gather some palm roots."

99

"I reckon I'll have to look inside. General wants to know everything what comes in, and everything what goes out."

Jem sighed. He should have just told the truth.

"Oh, go on," Juba said. "I'm not so old that I don't remember what it was like to be a boy. I've made plenty of mistakes myself. Just make certain you set him out afore you put anything else in there."

"How'd you—"

Juba grinned. "Never seen a body tote an empty basket with such care. Never heard a basket squawk like that, neither."

"I was hoping Phaedra wouldn't have to know about this," Jem said.

"You're not starting more trouble, are you?" Juba's expression turned stern. "We already got plenty of that."

"No, sir," Jem said. "I promise."

Juba softened. "I'll not tell. But I'm off sentry duty in a couple hours. Best be back before then."

"Thank you." With a glance over his shoulder, Jem passed through the gate.

"What you gonna do with it?" Juba called.

"Teach him to fly," Jem said.

Juba's laughter followed Jem to the edge of the forest. He stopped to peer into the trees, reminding himself that obia didn't attack in daytime. A young dove flitted from branch to branch above him—a sure sign that Omen would learn to fly this day. Jem breathed in the pine-scented air.

He found a sassafras seedling and crushed one of its leaves. The sharp, clean scent reminded him of Aunt Winnie and all the times she'd doctored the sick with a tea she made from sassafras roots. "Searches the blood for what's ailing," she'd say, "and goes to work on it." He wondered what sassafras tea could do for an owlet's blood. Should he have tried to mix a potion to heal Omen's wing?

Jem set the basket down and took the buckskin sleeve from under his shirt. He rubbed the blue beads three times for protection, then fastened the sleeve to his right forearm.

"Here we are," he said, and lifted the lid. The owlet glared up at him and clacked his beak. "I'm sorry for the rough ride."

Jem turned the basket on its side, and Omen marched out. He stretched his wings, then folded them back as he took in the surroundings with quick turns of his head.

"I know you must be vexed," Jem said. "Didn't mean to keep you in there so long. I'd be afeared, too, if I was you. Was when I first came here. But I got used to it. Even learned to like it."

If Omen had any misgivings about being back at the scene of his near-death, Jem couldn't tell. The owlet charged along a path through the brush. Jem followed, wondering why he hadn't thought of this earlier. But although Omen chased a chameleon through a thicket and chastised a robin, he seemed content to do so from the ground, hopping along and then surging ahead as fast as his too-big feet would carry him, body leaning forward precariously.

When the owlet hopped onto a stump that had fallen over the path, Jem got an idea. "Come here," he called, and held out his arm.

Omen wasn't interested. He'd been distracted by a butterfly flitting among the tree trunks, its yellow wings glowing like a star in the dim light.

"You can catch him if you try," Jem told him. "Go on." But the butterfly quickly darted out of sight and he was able to get Omen to climb onto the buckskin sleeve.

Jem walked even deeper into the forest, looking for a low branch. When he came to a fallen tree with its broken trunk resting at chest level, he put his arm out so Omen could step onto the bark.

Before he could coax the owlet to spread his wings, Omen took off after a large beetle running along the trunk. He caught it and swallowed it in one gulp.

"Fly down," Jem called, flapping his arms. "You can do it."

Omen just stared at him.

Jem groaned. At this rate, Omen would never learn.

"Watch me." Jem began to run about, weaving in and out of the trees.

The fresh smell of the pine and the lilt of birdsong and crickets made him light-headed. With every flap of his arms, the weight of his troubles eased off a bit, as though all he had to do was wave them away.

Omen didn't seem impressed. He closed one eye and stretched his neck forward, opening his beak.

A pellet dropped onto the pine needles.

Jem ducked under the trunk to take a look. He'd gotten into the habit of examining Omen's castings. He'd collected all kinds of skeletons from creatures the owlet had consumed: lizards, fish, and the occasional mouse. The bones were so tiny, it was often difficult to see them.

When he looked up, the owlet was no longer on the trunk.

Jem searched the ground, but the colors of the needles, trunks, and underbrush made spotting Omen difficult. The owlet blended into the forest, as though he were a part of it, and his feathers were specially crafted to make him invisible against the leaves and bark.

A shriek came from behind a saw palmetto. There he was, chasing a frog.

"Here, look." Jem opened the pouch and held out a crawfish he'd caught in the stream. The owlet gulped it down and demanded more with plaintive cries.

"Not until you fly." Jem lifted him back onto the branch.

Omen sulked. He wouldn't look at Jem until he offered another crawfish.

"Flap your wings," Jem said, waving his arms to show what he meant.

This time the owlet obliged.

"Now you're getting it."

But Omen stopped. Maybe all he needed was a little push. Jem coaxed him onto his sleeve and climbed from the fallen tree to a wide oak bough a few feet away. From there he was able to set him onto a higher branch.

But the stubborn bird just stood there, shifting on his feet.

"Don't be scared," Jem said. He was certain that once he felt the air under his wings, Omen's natural owl instincts would take over.

The owlet glared at him.

Jem reached up and shook the branch ever so gently. Omen squawked, turning his head to look.

Jem gave the branch a harder shove. Omen wailed and lost his footing, tumbling headfirst to the ground.

"Omen!" Jem cried, scrambling down after him. What kind of teacher was he? He was no better than the crows! At least the owlet was standing, his eyes open. "I'm sorry."

But Omen wouldn't look at him. Was it Jem's imagination, or did the hurt wing now fold at an odd angle?

When Jem tried to get him back into the basket, the owlet snapped at him.

He finally laid it on its side and lured Omen in with a salamander he found under a mossy rock.

As he pushed the lid down, the owlet cried out. *Whooo, whooo, whooo!*

Who, indeed.

Finally Omen settled down and grew quiet. Jem headed back toward Mose, wondering what kind of person would push his only friend out of a tree. Ducking under the overhanging branches, he heard a strange whistling, as though the wind itself scolded him for what he'd done.

Chapter Sixteen

November 5, 1739

It took him two days, three tree frogs, a chameleon, and a small mouse to buy Omen's forgiveness. During that time, making up with the owlet occupied all of Jem's free moments and most of his energy.

When Domingo showed up one morning with two spears, Jem couldn't resist the chance to take a break.

"Can I go hunting with Domingo for a while?" he asked Phaedra. "We won't be gone for long."

Phaedra grumbled at first, but then her gaze fell on the empty basket where the corn had been kept and she fell silent. There had been no ship from Spain or Cuba and the food stores were dwindling. With the men drilling constantly and up half the night on watch, there hadn't been meat in the stew pot for days.

Omen watched the boys from his perch, eyes following Jem all the way to the gate.

He and Domingo turned east and headed across the field where the militia drilled. The sun was high and the men broke from formation and headed to the shade at the tree line.

Big Sunday's jaw set as they approached. A look Jem couldn't cipher crossed the man's face as he gazed at his son. Was he vexed that Domingo was spending the afternoon in the forest with Jem? As they passed, Big Sunday said something in Domingo's language. Domingo laughed.

"What'd he say?" Jem asked.

"To be careful."

"What's so funny about that?"

"He also said to try not to find any more owls."

They were just inside the trees when they heard Rojas speaking to Big Sunday. "A pity your boy is Indian."

"Why's that?" Big Sunday asked.

"Well…" The general coughed. "A lazy people, no? No offense to your dead wife, of course."

Domingo stopped short and turned back to listen.

"You think my son is lazy?" asked Big Sunday.

"It's just…" The general seemed to search for the right words. "The Indians are unreliable."

Domingo bent his head. Jem touched Domingo's arm, wanting to pull him forward, away from the hateful talk. But Domingo grasped his wrist and held it fast.

"What do you mean?" Big Sunday's tone had gone flat. Jem wondered if the general knew what dangerous ground he was treading.

The general sighed. "Your boy doesn't stand beside you. In the militia."

"Why would he join the militia?"

"You are his papa, no? Is this not why he is called Domingo?"

"My son was never a slave," Big Sunday said. "He has no reason to join the militia."

"Of course. But a son should stand with his father. The Indians are like children, no? They have no loyalty."

Jem shifted under the discomfort of his friend's shame.

"What loyalty does my son owe to the Spanish?" Big Sunday asked.

"I'm surprised you say such things when you yourself have the king and the people of St. Augustine to thank for your freedom."

"My son was born free. He owes no such debt."

Jem gazed at Domingo. Was this why he lived in his mother's village instead of at Mose? What did that feel like—to be born free? Domingo let go of Jem's arm, concentrating on the men's words.

"H…how can you say this?" the general sputtered. "My king saved your son's people from the fires of hell and protects them to this day."

"Your king could never repay what his salvation has cost my son's people. St. Augustine wouldn't be here today without the help of Domingo's ancestors."

Jem glanced over at Domingo again, but his expression was hidden by the shadow of a pine bough.

"Those are sacrilegious and treasonous words, Captain," the general warned. "You forget yourself."

"I forget nothing." Big Sunday let out a breath. "I'm grateful for your king's sanctuary, but it's not charity." Jem recognized the bland, slow enunciation of syllables Big Sunday often used when he was holding back anger. "My liberty was purchased. To be paid for with my last drop of blood, if it comes to that."

"I should say so," the general said. "See that you don't forget."

"There's something you would do well to remember," Big Sunday said. "The Indians and the people of Mose are all that stand between you and the English. You need us as much as we need you. Mayhap, even more."

"You think I'm afraid of the English?" The general laughed. "The Spanish are the finest soldiers in all of Christendom."

"Then we have nothing to worry about," Big Sunday said.

"Only the unpredictability of the savages."

Whoosh! Domingo's spear flew through the air.

"No!" Jem cried.

It landed not a foot from where Rojas stood. The sharp point had pierced the ground at a sunny spot near the edge of the trees.

Jem stood in stunned silence, not sure which surprised him more: that Domingo had thrown his spear at the general, or that he'd missed.

"Your boy tried to kill me!" The general's face was ashen.

Domingo stood, his eyes on the place where the spear had landed. In the distance, the faint tolling of the church bell called the faithful to Mass.

Big Sunday walked over and pulled the spear from the ground. He whistled softly and knelt to examine the spot.

When Big Sunday stood, there was something in his hand. At first, Jem thought it was a vine or fallen branch. But when he took a few steps closer, he realized it wasn't.

Big Sunday held up a snake, still writhing. The tip of Domingo's spear had severed the head from the body.

A breeze from the marsh brought the sulphury scent of low tide. Jem breathed it in, taking comfort in the solid, earthy smell.

The general opened his mouth as if to speak, then closed it. Staring at the carcass, he ran a hand over the top of his head.

The snake's tail rattled faintly. Jem shivered.

In the distance, on the trail between Mose and St. Augustine, an approaching horse kicked up a cloud of dust.

Domingo stepped out from the stand of trees and Big Sunday handed him his spear and the body of the snake. The men in the militia rose from under the shade tree to stand at attention.

"Can I have the rattle?" Jem asked.

Domingo severed it with one swipe of his knife and handed it to Jem. "Let's go," he said and headed back into the forest.

"Wait," Jem called. There was something foreboding about the crouch of the incoming rider and the speed of the horse.

"Maybe he's here to tell us the king's ship has come in," one of the men joked.

"We'd be last to hear about that," another said.

"Silence!" the general ordered.

The militia gathered around as the rider stopped in front of Big Sunday and the general, his horse rearing from the sudden pull on his reins.

"What news have you?" the general demanded.

"The governor would have you know..." The rider's throat bobbed as though he'd swallowed a musket ball and couldn't quite get it down. "The treaty with England has been broken!"

"Am I to understand—?" Rojas began.

"*Sí. La guerra!*" the rider cried. "War!"

Chapter Seventeen

January 23, 1740

W e're at war," Jem reminded Phaedra as she rubbed at the mud behind his ears with a wet cloth.

"White men ain't happy unless they at war. That, or telling folks what to do. It's their nature," she said. "I wouldn't give neither their war nor their telling a second thought if I wasn't stuck out here between them."

Since war had been declared, the priest from St. Augustine came more frequently, requiring daily prayers and devotions. Phaedra demanded Jem be clean and neatly dressed for the priest's visits. But she shook her head as he left. "All the praying in the world ain't gonna keep the English away."

Wispy gray clouds hung low over Mose, like the moss hanging from the oaks. Most of the men and some of the women had been sent to work on the Castillo. Rotted beams needed replacing. The gun deck was being reinforced with layer upon layer of tabby mortar to support the weight of the additional cannons, sent from Cuba last year to better protect St. Augustine from the encroaching English.

"I should lend a hand at the Castillo," Jem said.

"What could you do?" Phaedra didn't even look up from collecting acorns.

"I could mix tabby, or—"

"With those puny arms? You'd just get in the way. Besides, who'd look after that creature?"

Jem swallowed a mouthful of guilt. He hadn't had much time to find food for Omen lately. Any fish he caught went to the stew pot, not to hungry owls.

"Step lighter," she added. "You're crushing the acorns."

"I can't help it. They're all over."

"Everywhere but in your basket." Phaedra peered at the few Jem had collected.

"You'd be better off with the general's daughter helping you," he said. "She wouldn't step on nearly so many. Even if she did, she's too light to break them."

"I don't want that girl around," Phaedra snapped. "Ain't natural her being over here. Ought to stay in St. Augustine among her own people."

"But the general is her people." Jem stooped to scoop up another handful of acorns.

"Hush."

Ping. Something hard hit his head and bounced off. He glanced at Phaedra, but she was bent over her basket. "That man ain't people," she said.

The next day, Jem gathered some beetles and a chameleon and shut them up in one of Phaedra's baskets. Omen wailed from the roof of the chosa where he'd climbed to oversee the preparations.

"Come down, you feathered fusspot," Jem teased.

There was a stirring above, then *whoosh!* Omen swooped down on Jem, digging his talons into his scalp. Jem dropped the basket, the lid came off, and the chameleon darted toward the shelter of Phaedra's drying rack.

Omen lifted off of Jem's head. With a couple of beats, he was over the chameleon, wings flapping furiously.

Jem's eyes swam, whether with pain or pride, he wasn't sure. He felt weightless himself, as though he could rise up beside Omen and sail with him. "You're flying!" he cheered. "Huzzah!"

The problem was, Omen didn't know how to land. He slammed into the ground and fell backward, feet sticking out. The chameleon disappeared up the post and into the drying sweetgrass. Phaedra cackled at the sight.

Omen struggled to his feet, put his head down, and tucked his wings tight around his body. He strutted toward the watchtower, hunger forgotten.

Phaedra chuckled even harder.

"Stop," Jem said. "Can't you see he doesn't like to be laughed at?"

"Fancy that," she said. "I've wounded the poor critter's feelings."

"How'd you have liked it if folks laughed at you when you were learning to walk?"

"Probably did," she said. "I disremember."

Omen was struggling to climb onto his perch. When Jem tried to lift him, Omen snapped at his hand.

"I'm sorry," Jem said. "And don't pay any attention to Phaedra."

Omen wouldn't be comforted.

What if he decided not to try flying again? Jem had to think of something quick. "Have I told you how Brother Rabbit got Fox's tail for the Sky God?"

Omen blinked and turned his glare on Jem. *Good,* he thought. *At least he's interested.* Jem was sure it wasn't just people who liked stories. Owls liked them too.

Jem lowered his voice to the almost whisper that seemed to entrance Omen.

Fox was always trying to put one over on the other creatures. But he met his match in Brother Rabbit.

One day, Fox stole corn from Bear's den, and Bear meant to get even.

As he ran through the forest looking for a place to hide, Fox came upon Brother Rabbit.

"Help me hide," he begged.

"You're about the color of Squirrel," Brother Rabbit said. "He's not at home now and you could fit in his tree."

Bear was getting closer, and since he couldn't think of

anything better, Fox climbed into Squirrel's tree. And with only the tip of his tail showing, he looked just like Squirrel.

"You see Fox?" Bear asked Brother Rabbit.

"Not presently," he said. "Ask Squirrel."

Bear saw what he thought was Squirrel's tail sticking out of the tree. "You seen Fox?" he asked.

"He's not here," Fox called in his best imitation of Squirrel.

"Climb up higher and look," Bear ordered.

But Fox was stuck. He tried to get loose, but it was no use. Bear got mad and started tugging at his tail, "I said, get up there and look."

But Fox couldn't move. Bear tugged harder and harder.

Fox's tail came off in his hands. When he realized it was Fox, Bear clawed at the tree until it broke open. Fox began running again, this time with Bear at his heels.

Brother Rabbit admired Fox's fine tail as he picked it up off the ground.

Omen did his cry that sounded like a dog barking.

Was he trying to tell a story of his own? Did creatures tell stories? Did big owls tell them to little owls and make the little ones work out what they meant? The blast of a horn sounded from the top of the watchtower. Wings flapping, Omen rose about two feet into the air and flew to the drying rack, where he landed unsteadily on a mound of sweetgrass.

"Coming in from the north!" the sentry shouted.

Jem ripped his gaze from Omen to the north wall of the fort.

"To arms! To arms!"

Some members of the militia worked to secure the gate, while others rushed to get their muskets. Had the English troops finally arrived? Jem climbed the lower rungs of the watchtower ladder to get a better look. A rider had already set out for St. Augustine.

At first, he couldn't see the approaching soldiers. The trail that stretched to the north was empty, the fields around littered with the stumps of broken cornstalks. The only movement he saw was birds hopping among them, hunting for grubs in the turned soil.

Then they appeared in the distance. But if this was how the English fought a war, Jem could see why Rojas was cocky. There were only three of them. As ragged a detachment as Jem had ever seen, staggering like crabs in a circle, muskets drawn to cover the surrounding territory.

One of the men must have spied the militia's guns peeking out over the walls of Mose, for suddenly the three dropped their weapons and began waving and shouting.

"Stand down!" the sentry shouted. The gates swung open and a party of six militiamen, led by Big Sunday, surged through, muskets drawn and at the ready.

Soon they returned, supporting the newcomers. Who were they? They were white men, but didn't look like the English soldiers in Charles Town. Their shirts and trousers were torn and stained, and they carried nothing but small packs and muskets.

Big Sunday's face was drawn. "They're Spanish."

"Where'd they come from?" Thomas asked.

"Fort Picolata," Big Sunday said.

"Where's that?" Thomas asked.

"West of St. Augustine," Big Sunday said. "On the St. Johns River."

Adine handed each man a jug of water. They drank until it ran down their faces, leaving trails like gray veins down their throats.

One of the men spoke to Big Sunday in rapid Spanish. Jem recognized a few words. *Todos* meant "all," and *fuego* was "fire."

"We need to get them to the governor," Big Sunday said.

"What happened?" Juba asked.

The man spoke urgently, anguish twisting his features. He handed the jug back to Adine and began to gesticulate, arms wide, pointing here and there. When he finished, he dropped his face into his hands.

"He's a captain," Big Sunday relayed. "He and the others left the fort to hunt. The English must have come soon after. By the time they got back, there was nothing they could do. They hid in the woods, listening to the screams of their fellows as the English set fire to the fort."

Jem's throat ached. The smell of smoke still clung to the soldiers' ragged clothes. *What could it have been like to be there? Stuck out in the woods. Powerless to save your friends.* He gripped the handle of his knife, nails digging into his palm.

"There's more." Big Sunday shook his head. "Soon as the English were done, they crossed the river and took Fort Pupa.

Didn't burn it. These soldiers saw the English flag flying there before they set out for St. Augustine."

"Rider coming!" the sentry called.

It was Rojas. He made the men repeat their story as he sat on his horse, towering above them. When they finished, he barked his orders. "Prepare the cart and take them to the governor."

"What does this mean?" Tildy asked.

"It means the English control the St. Johns River." Big Sunday said.

"It means we won't have long to wait now," Phaedra muttered.

Chapter Eighteen

February 28, 1740

The English still hadn't arrived, and neither had the promised supplies from Spain. The soldiers in St. Augustine hadn't been paid in months. Worry spread like a brushfire through the marsh grass to Mose.

"The king will make certain we get a shipment," Jem said when Phaedra grumbled over the last of the yams. "It's part of the bargain he made with us."

"You believe the King of Spain cares about us?" she said. "He doesn't even give a fig about his own people over here. That governor can prance around in his blue jacket and silk stockings all day long, but it doesn't change the truth."

"What truth?" Jem couldn't help but ask.

"Governor's nothing but a fancy scarecrow. Here to keep the English from having at the treasure ships as they sail to Spain to fill the King's coffers with gold and silver. Those ships get through, don't they?"

"I'm sure the supplies will come," Jem said. "They'll get here before the English."

"English already headed this way," Phaedra predicted. "Gonna come land on our heads, just like yon birdlet."

———

The setting sun was casting a red glow over the eastern wall of the fort when Jem heard a whistle at the gate.

Reynard led his mule Celeste into the yard. Instead of his usual hide hat, he wore a red fur cap at a jaunty angle.

Jem studied it. "That possum fur?"

"Indeed it is. King of England himself wears one. Keeps his head warmer than a golden crown."

"You're fooling," Jem said.

"I assure you I am not. I know all about the king. Some of the Cherokees I trade with up north traveled over the sea to meet him about ten years back. They had dinner at his palace and gave him a red fur cap just like this."

"How'd you get it so red?"

"Dyed it with elderberry mash."

"Wish I had a hat like that," Jem said. "Don't care for the English king, but I sure would like something to keep my ears warm on chilly nights."

"What about that hide I traded you?" Reynard asked. "Thought you'd make a cap of that."

"Had to use it for an owl sleeve. I've gone back to wearing my palm hat."

"What have you to trade this time?"

"I saved some of Omen's baby feathers," Jem said. He fetched them from the chosa and held them out for Reynard's inspection.

"Not much of a market for these," Reynard said. "The darker, stronger feathers are what the northern tribes value. Got to carry what my customers want, you know."

"I see." Jem tried to hide his disappointment as he stuffed the feathers into his pocket and took out the whistle he'd been working on. "I haven't had time to make any more whistles for trading. This one's for owl calls." He handed it to Reynard.

The trader ran his fingers over the whistle. Jem had carved two crude feathered horns at the top of the hollow reed and two wings into the sides.

"Fine work," said Reynard.

Jem had tried doing owl calls himself, but he had discovered that blowing through a hollow stick made a sound much closer to Omen's cries.

Reynard reached over and pretended to pull something from behind Jem's ear. "What have we here?"

He held up a flat piece of glass about the size of a coin. Jem held it to his eye, but it was too thick to see through. "What is it?"

"Magnifier glass. Lets you examine things up close. Look." He took the glass piece and held it in front of the carving on the whistle.

Jem peered through the glass. Each cut his knife had made in the surface of the wood looked enormous. Reynard moved the glass to the feather. Every individual barb showed clearly. Jem was amazed. Surely something like this would bring its owner good luck. "It's wonderful," Jem said. "But I've nothing to trade for it."

"I'm not worried about that. I got it for you special," Reynard said. "Consider it a gift between friends." He put the glass in Jem's palm and winked. "Perhaps someday you will find a way to repay me."

"Thank you," Jem said, slipping the charmed glass into his pocket. "Wish I could use it to make the food stores larger."

Reynard regarded him with concern. "I know times are hard here. You look hungry. Are you afraid?"

Jem considered the question. "Some say supplies won't get through in time, but I know the king won't let his subjects starve."

"No, I'm sure you're right about that. Still, I heard some people are ready to leave and take their chances elsewhere."

"Who?" Jem asked. The men in the militia might grumble, but they had taken a vow of loyalty. "Not anyone at Mose?"

"Probably just idle talk," Reynard assured him. "Have they put you to work over at the Castillo?"

Jem clenched his jaw. "Wish they had. I've been stuck here gathering fern heads and digging up palm roots for the cook pot."

"I heard they have scores of cannons over there. Too many to count."

"Naw, they say there's only about twenty," Jem said. "Hope I'll get to see them soon."

"I'm sure you will," Reynard said. "I was hoping to get in there myself. Wanted to make some trades before it gets too dangerous around these parts. But the guards won't let me in. Looks like I'll have to leave here with a full pack."

As Reynard let Celeste away, Jem took out the glass and

held it over a beetle he'd caught for Omen. Its black wings weren't black at all, but a shimmering mixture of black, red, purple, and blue.

"I'll find a way to pay you back!" he shouted to Reynard.

"I know you will," the trader called over his shoulder.

A few days later, Jem was in the yard outside the chosa examining his collection through the glass. The snake's rattle was his new favorite. Its surface had a shiny appearance like a fingernail, but not as thick.

"I don't care if it is bad luck," he heard Phaedra shout at Omen. "I'm gonna knock you out and pluck you myself if you do it again!"

The owl's latest trick was to land on Phaedra's baskets. Jem couldn't blame him, really. Some of them were just the right size and shape for a nice owl's nest. Did he remember his old home in the pine tree?

Omen squawked at Phaedra from his perch on the watchtower before flying over to inspect Jem's collection. Bored by the remnants of his own castings, he turned his attention to the drying rack.

"What are you looking for?" Jem asked Omen. "Have you found an interesting bug?" He held the glass over the sweetgrass, searching for what had caught the owl's attention. A spider was hard at work, spinning a delicate web. Fascinated, Jem watched as the tiny threads formed an intricate pattern.

A thin finger of smoke began to rise from the pile of brown grass. Omen shifted uneasily, then flew off. At first Jem didn't realize what was happening. Then he saw that the glass concentrated and focused the beam of sunlight, creating intense heat. Suddenly a small flame sprang up.

Jem let it rise for a moment, watching it spread to the surrounding strands. When it leapt greedily, he tried to blow it out, but his breath only fed the flames.

The fire quickly spread through the dry grass and onto the supports of the rack. Jem scanned the yard for something to put it out. There was nothing in sight. He ran to the chosa for his blanket, but by the time he got back, Phaedra had appeared with a bucket of water.

She threw water onto the flames, and a wall of smoke rose from the ruined grass.

"What are you trying to do?" she cried, thrusting the bucket at Jem's gut. "It's not enough we gotta starve? Now you're trying to burn this place down around us?"

Chapter Nineteen

March 31, 1740

P ack more in!" Big Sunday yelled. They were lined up in the rain outside the north wall of Fort Mose, each holding a bucket of clay.

"We gonna wash away, just like in that story the priest told about Noah and the ark," Phaedra said. "Except Mose ain't gonna float."

Jem ignored her. Despite being drenched to the bone and shivery, he was grateful to have something to do that took him out of the cramped and miserable chosa. He preferred slapping clay on the damaged wall to crouching in the damp hut hour after hour.

Spring had come, bringing not English troops, but rain. Days of bone-chilling, spirit-soaking, mildew-growing rain. It came down so hard that the seeds planted in the muddy fields washed away. No charcoal could be made; the wood was waterlogged and wouldn't burn. Despite the looming threat of war, the blacksmiths could forge no more weapons without charcoal.

The creek rose, inching closer and closer to Mose, until its waters licked at the fort's walls and seeped into its foundations. The meager remains of the winter stores grew life again. A powdery green and blue mold covered the grain like a dusty blanket.

When the rain let up for a few days and warm air dried the roofs and fields, Mose faced another problem.

Mosquitoes. They descended like a cloud, their whine a constant chorus in the ear. There was fear of fever.

Smudge pits were dug, filled with dried corn cobs, and set afire to discourage the mosquitoes. They smoldered day and night, filling the air with smoke that stung Jem's eyes.

After a while Jem had to remind himself that they were at war. At first he'd awakened every morning sure that this would be the day the English would come. He'd prepared by sharpening his knife regularly and hoarding what extra food he could scavenge. He even kept a supply of beetles and chameleons at the ready for Omen. But as the days became weeks, the possibility of an attack became more and more remote. At first he was confused, then he'd gotten bored.

There'd been no news of the English since the northern forts were taken. The governor had sent a messenger to Havana. No word had come back. He sent another messenger. St. Augustine was desperate for workers and food. But it was as though the rain clouds themselves washed away the governor's letters begging for help. Even the messengers had disappeared.

Rojas rode into Mose in a fury one afternoon. Mud kicked up by his galloping horse covered the back of the general's blue jacket and boots. "Ring the bell!" he ordered.

As he waited for people to gather, Rojas paced the yard, stomping at puddles.

Jem couldn't imagine what had gotten him so upset.

"The English," the governor finally said, "dogs that they are and always will be, have gathered up a sorry fleet of ships and sent them to the waters off Anastasia Island."

Jem tried to hide his excitement. Finally, something was happening! He glanced at Big Sunday, who stood with his hands at his sides, gaze on the ground. A vein on his forehead bulged, giving him away. The thrill Jem had felt vanished. It was bad news.

"What does this mean?" Juba asked.

"It means that it is more important than ever that we crush them and send them back to their little island," the general said.

What kind of charm would Aunt Winnie design against the English, Jem wondered. He just might have to make one of his own.

"It means they've blockaded the harbor." Big Sunday's voice was tight. "None of those ships or supplies the king promised will be coming."

The rain made it made it difficult for Omen to fly. He spent most of his time perched in the shelter of the watchtower, surveying the drenched yard. It also made it hard for Jem to keep up with the owl's appetite. Luckily, there were plenty of worms. Driven out of the drenched earth, they were easy to collect, but it took a lot of earthworms to satisfy an owl.

Omen was fully grown now. He needed to learn to hunt.

One morning after the rains had finally stopped, Jem found a drowned rat in a bucket. It was fairly small, but just right for his purposes. He pulled some fiber from palm fronds and tied the ends together to make decent length of string. He fastened one end around the rat's neck, hid the rodent under Phaedra's drying rack, and spooled out the string so that it extended past the corner of the chosa.

Then he waited.

Finally, the wind shifted and Omen abandoned the watchtower in favor of the roof.

Jem walked casually past Omen and around the hut. He could feel the owl's eyes on him. Once out of Omen's sight, Jem stretched flat in the dirt. Carefully he pulled the string, drawing the dead rat from under the drying rack into the open.

But when Jem peeked, Omen was grooming his wing feathers with his beak.

Jem jerked the string and made squeaking rat noises as he pulled still more.

He peeked again. Omen had lifted his wings.

Now we're getting somewhere. Dive, Omen!

But instead of diving, Omen rose and flew off toward the watchtower.

Tildy and Adine ducked as the owl passed over their heads.

"That bird's a menace!" Tildy declared. As she turned, she must have caught sight of the rat out of the corner of her eye. Her scream was loud enough to have been heard in St. Augustine.

Jem dragged the dead rat toward him. But before he could pull it out of sight, Phaedra rounded the corner and stepped right on the limp body.

"Get this carcass out of here!" she screeched. "What are you doing messing with vermin, you fool? Don't you know they carry disease? And get me some grass while you're out there!"

As he was returning from the marsh, Jem saw Omen fly past with something gripped in his talons. After all the trouble he'd gone through—and gotten into—had Omen have learned to hunt on his own?

"Looks as if Omen's learned to hunt," he announced when he got back to the yard.

"Fine hunter, indeed," Phaedra muttered.

"What do you mean?"

"Go see what he caught and then tell me if you still believe he's learned to hunt."

Omen had landed at the base of the watchtower and was guarding his catch fiercely, strutting around making warning calls that sounded more like barks. All Jem could see was that the owl had caught something brownish. Was it a rabbit or a squirrel?

Jem edged closer. If he could get a look at the head or tail, he'd be able to tell which. It didn't take long to see it was neither.

The owl's prey was a dried-up chunk of cow dung.

Jem could hear Phaedra and the others over at the cook fire laughing. Let them joke about it. He didn't care. Omen might not be a skilled hunter, but it was a start.

Later that week, the owl brought home a shrew. A few days after that, a bat. He swallowed the shrew whole, but pulled the bat apart, dropping the wings under his perch.

"Get that nastiness out of my sight!" Phaedra jabbed the air with her horn nail, making Jem step away. "And then get water for the stew. We'll all starve while you crawl around in the dirt playing with that bird."

Jem had hoped that Omen would bring home a bigger catch, or at least one more appealing to add to the stew pot. With all hands at the Castillo or in the fields, there'd been little time to fish. "I could ask Domingo to show me how to trap," he offered.

"You think you're gonna go out there and run around in the woods? Ha!" Phaedra was more ill-tempered than ever these days; she barely let Jem out of her sight. All day they worked in the fields side by side, tending to the sickly corn plants that had been saved from the rain or planting new ones started with the last of the remaining seed. Or they dug palm roots and collected fern heads. Evenings they did the chores left undone by those working at the Castillo.

Jem gave up on the notion of hunting. He didn't have time anyway. What with gathering wood for the fire, fetching water, grinding acorns, and finding critters for Omen, he was occupied every moment of the day. By sundown, he had trouble keeping his eyes open. And Phaedra was always looking over his shoulder, criticizing every step he took.

Back in Charles Town, Aunt Winnie had powerful charms to protect her. She even made charms to keep unwanted people away.

If only he had one against Phaedra.

Chapter Twenty

April 21, 1740

W hat in creation?" Phaedra shot out of her bed, waking Jem from a deep sleep.

Sitting up, he became aware of the overpowering stench that had roused Phaedra. He rushed outside to find that the very charm he'd wished for had fallen to earth as though a gift from the Sky God himself.

It was a rather small, quite dead, and extremely smelly skunk. And it hadn't exactly fallen out of the sky. Omen held it tightly in his talons.

Phaedra was at his heels. "Get rid of that thing before we all expire."

But Omen didn't want to let it go, so Jem waited for him to finish his meal. Owls must not have much of a sense of smell, he figured.

Tildy came over to see what the fuss was about. She took one look at the owl's feast and exclaimed that she had lost her appetite.

"Good," Phaedra said. "The pot's empty anyway."

Finally, Omen dropped what was left of the carcass. Jem wrapped it in a wide palm leaf and stashed it under a pile of rocks. After a sparse breakfast of thin gruel, he fetched the packet and headed to the Indian village. He'd ask Domingo to show him how to tan the skunk's hide.

The streets were even more empty than usual. He finally found Domingo sitting on a rock by the creek that ran between the village and St. Augustine. He was whittling a thin plank of wood about as long as his arm and as wide as his wrist.

"Where is everyone?" Jem asked. "Over at the Castillo?"

"Mostly." Domingo shrugged. "Some have gone."

"Gone where?"

"West…or south." Domingo said.

"Why'd they do that?"

"To get ahead of the English. Last time they came, they took prisoners from here and sold them as slaves. Time before that, they burned the village to the ground."

"Why'd they do that?" Jem asked. "What have your people ever done to them?"

Domingo shrugged. "Friend to England's enemy. When the English attack us, they weaken the Spanish hold on these lands."

"But these are the lands of your ancestors!" Jem said, his voice rising with indignation. "By rights, you're the ones who should hold them."

"No one owns the land," Domingo said quietly. "People are of the land, not over it."

"Were you here when they burned the village?" Jem asked.

Domingo nodded, his jaw muscles tightening the way Big Sunday's did when he was angry. "I was small," he said, "but I remember. We hid in the woods until they left. My parents made plans to leave after that, but we never did."

"Why not?"

"My father decided he must stay to fight the English. He started the militia with other maroons. Led them to Carolina to help others escape. He told my mother he owed it to those still enslaved."

This was a story Jem hadn't heard. "What did your mother say?"

"I do not know. During Father's first trip back north, yellow fever took half the village. My mother was first to die."

"I'm sorry." Jem didn't know what else to say. He'd started out thinking how unfair it was that the English kept grabbing up more and more territory. Then it occurred to him that it wasn't fair for the Spanish to rule here instead of Domingo's people. Now he just felt sad, not angry.

Domingo went back to his whittling. "Why do you carry that?" he asked, nodding toward the pine leaf packet. "It stinks something awful."

"A skunk carcass. Can you show me how to tan the hide?"

"Smell won't come out with tanning."

"Don't want it to." Jem smiled. "Not all of it, anyway." He told Domingo what he had in mind.

"No need to tan the hide," Domingo advised. "Just keep the tail."

Jem hadn't thought of that. It seemed like a good idea. He used his knife to cut off the tail and buried the carcass at the edge of the trees.

Clouds, glowing orange-pink like the inside of a conch shell, clustered on the eastern horizon. Echoes of shouts and pounding carried across the water from the Castillo.

"They didn't let you work over yonder either?" Jem asked.

Domingo raised his eyebrows. "Plenty to do here."

"Do you ever think about leaving?"

"Many times," Domingo said. The tight line on his jaw came back, and although Jem wanted to ask more questions, he didn't feel right about it.

"What are you making?" Jem studied the wood plank. "Some kind of a trap?"

"*Atlatl*," Domingo said.

"At what?" Jem asked.

Domingo pronounced the word slowly. "*At-la-tul.*"

"What's it for?"

"Spear throwing."

"For hunting?"

Domingo hesitated for a moment. "Yes." He went back to his whittling.

Jem had never seen anything like the strange object in Domingo's hands. One of the ends was narrow and two semicircular indentations had been cut into the wood. At the other end, Domingo had gouged a groove along the surface. He carved a bit longer, then brushed off the shavings and picked up a long spear. Resting the point of the spear in the creek, Domingo slid the other end into the groove on the atlatl. It fit perfectly.

"What does it do?" Jem asked.

Domingo stepped off the rock and faced east. He grasped the end using the semicircular cutouts as a handle. He raised the atlatl and spear over his head and brought them back as though he were going to throw them. Holding the atlatl tight in his right hand, Domingo swung it in a wide arc over his head and lunged as he released the spear.

The spear flew through the air as though shot from a cannon. It soared farther and faster than Jem would have imagined possible, landing in the bank about a quarter mile down the creek.

"Can I try?" he asked.

Domingo handed him another spear.

Jem tried to imitate Domingo's stance.

"Like this." Domingo helped him fit the spear into the groove. "Now."

Jem launched it with as much force as he could, but he felt off balance and awkward. And although the spear went farther than if he'd thrown it without the atlatl, it still traveled only a fraction of the distance Domingo had achieved before landing with a splash in the creek.

"Again," Domingo said. He handed Jem another spear.

Jem tried three more times. Each time, the spear traveled farther.

"Can I borrow a spear?" Jem asked. "And an atlatl?"

Jem finished the owl whistle. He lifted it to his lips and blew through the hollow core. *Whooo, whooo, whooo.* To his ears, it didn't sound much like an owl, but when he practiced from the other side of the fort, Omen hooted and circled three times before settling back on his perch. Satisfied, Jem put the whistle away and turned to his new project.

He was done with whistles. They were a trifle. The tools of the hunter were what he'd work on now. If he could provide more than just fish, he could make up for the trouble he'd caused and people would stop seeing him as a child.

He decided to make it his business to become skilled at using the atlatl. He closed his eyes and pictured himself in a dark clearing. A shadow moved in the distance, but this time he wasn't afraid. He swung the atlatl and lunged as the spear shot forward, whistling through the branches toward his target. It would take a while, but he could learn.

Every chance he got, Jem practiced with the atlatl. He finally got up the courage to demonstrate his new skill to Phaedra.

"Last thing we need is spears flying through the air," Phaedra declared. "We already got owls swooping at us. And that blasted creature stole my bonnet, right off the peg on the coop. Had to chase him with a broom before he'd drop it."

"He was just practicing," Jem said. Omen wouldn't have eaten her silly bonnet.

He was disappointed that she hadn't been impressed by his new weapon. Couldn't she see how useful his skill could be? What was she doing to help? The ladies in St. Augustine weren't buying baskets anymore. Why would they? Nothing to put in them. Not food, anyway. The governor had ordered all food be stored in the Castillo, even what they grew at Mose.

That evening it was too warm for a large fire, but the exhausted men who had worked at the Castillo until dark sat around the smudge pit eating a watered-down stew of fern heads, palm roots, and dried fish heads.

"I didn't bring my wife here to watch her starve," Thomas said.

"King don't care if we starve," Phaedra said, ladling a meager portion into Jem's bowl. "Long as we sit out here and protect St. Augustine. Bad enough his ships don't bring the supplies he promised. Now they're taking what we grow on our own!"

"You gonna tell the Rooster General we ain't giving up any of our crop?" Juba asked.

"We'll be all right." Big Sunday's voice carried so the others could hear. "Long as we pull together."

"Seems to me it's us doing all the pulling," Thomas said. "This isn't what we were promised."

Jem swallowed the last spoonful of his stew. He was still hungry. He pictured Aunt Winnie back in the kitchen of Master's house, roasting a tender hen over the fire. Did she ever think of him? He shook his head, trying to clear the memories.

Chapter Twenty-One

May 1, 1740

We shall bring the English to their knees!" Rojas promised from atop his horse. Despite the fact that there had been no battles, the general was full of boasts.

"I still think the governor should meet with the men from the Indian village," Big Sunday said. "They've fought the English before."

"Ha!" the general said. "You won't find many men left over there. They've all run off into the woods. I've no doubt one of them is wearing my blue pants!"

Big Sunday ignored the bizarre accusation. "Can't blame them," he said. "Last time the English came, they were the ones taken away in chains, not their Spanish allies."

The general glared at Big Sunday. "Remember your oath, Captain. And if stealing my uniform is part of a plot to shame me in front of the governor, I shall find the culprit!" He shook the horse's reins, dug his heels into its sides, and charged toward the gate.

"What's gotten into him?" Juba asked. "Does he really think someone stole his pants?"

"Fool probably left them somewhere," Phaedra said.

Adine snickered. "Gotten too big for his breeches, anyway, if you ask me."

But soon there was more than clothing missing.

The next morning, the cry woke Jem before first light. "Thomas! Tildy!" Phaedra called. Soon other voices joined hers, spreading out around the fort. Jem jumped out of bed and hurried outside.

"I woke and they were gone," Phaedra was telling Big Sunday.

"We've got to send the militia out to look for them," Adine said.

Big Sunday shook his head. "Did you look for their belongings?"

"Everything is gone," she said.

The knot in Jem's gut twisted tighter. Where had the blacksmith and his wife gone? Back to Pierce's place? He thought about Thomas and Tildy and the lie he'd told Pierce about them not wanting to stay at Mose. Had he been right? Or had he somehow conjured their leaving with his story? "Why?" he asked.

"I'll tell you why," Phaedra snapped. "So they won't have to face starvation and the English at the same time! They're smarter than all the rest of us!"

Jem waited for Big Sunday to tell Phaedra to hush, that she was wrong about Thomas and Tildy. That she was wrong about facing starvation and the English. That she didn't understand anything and that they were going to be all right.

But Big Sunday didn't say any of these things. He gazed at the gate and didn't say anything at all. And his silence worried Jem more than any words he'd ever heard.

＊ ＊

Whooo, whooo, whooo! Omen's hunting was taking him farther and farther outside the walls of the fort. Just the other day, Shadrack had reported seeing him in the forest near his kiln. Jem wondered if the owl had seen Thomas and Tildy leave. Though he was more and more a creature of the night, Omen always brought his catch back to the safety of the watchtower. From examining his castings under the magnifying glass, Jem could tell he was hunting larger game. The owl wasn't the only one. Jem had been hunting too.

He was waiting for a chance to sneak off to the forest again when Phaedra grabbed him by the shirtsleeve. "You've reeked of skunk for longer than I'd care to remember," she said. "Gimme that shirt, I'm gonna boil it in lye soap."

Too late, Jem tried to twist away. "Let go!" he cried. "You'll rip it."

"Give it over." She started to undo the buttons. He struggled to get free, but she held him fast.

"What in creation?" She pulled out the skunk tail he kept tucked in his pants waist.

"It's mine."

"No wonder you been stinking all this time! What'd you think, that this was one of those silly charms?" She slapped the back of his head.

A charm against you, he wanted to shout. *And it's been working!*

Phaedra wouldn't give the tail back. "You're not fit to live with civilized folk."

— —

"Where's the charcoal?" Big Sunday asked. The supply was already low because of the spring rains, and each new load was divided carefully between the forge and the Castillo.

"Turned to ash." Shadrack emptied his pockets. A few small pieces dropped onto the ground. "This is all that's left," he said.

Big Sunday stared at him. "How could you let that happen? How's the smith gonna forge blades without charcoal?"

"Got the misery in my head." Shadrack's eyes had a dull cast and were red around the lids.

"No more misery than the rest of us," Phaedra said. But she put a hand to his forehead. "You ain't got the fever, at least."

"Something coming for old Shadrack," he said. "Feel it in my back teeth."

"Only thing coming is the English and we won't be ready for them without new blades." Big Sunday glared at him.

"Where's your conjure bag?" Jem asked Shadrack. "It'll protect you."

141

The old man shook his head. "Gone. Hung it by my hut door while I tended the fire and the spirits done stole it back. I'm accursed."

"You think a bag of stink gonna protect you from the English?" Phaedra scoffed. "Stink don't bother them none. They wallow in it."

"You don't know nothing," Shadrack said.

"That may be, but I'm still here, ain't I? Didn't you say obia was coming for me? Here I am, obia!" Phaedra called. "Come and fetch me."

"Leave off!" Big Sunday barked. "Ain't no time for fooling. Shadrack, you take two men with you and get back out there and find enough wood to fire another load! We can't fight without charcoal and we can't survive without food. We don't have enough of either. Governor says our food stores won't last a month. We won't make it unless everyone does their part." Big Sunday drew a deep breath and exhaled loudly. "I shouldn't have said that. Keep it to yourselves. You and you go with him," he said, pointing to two of the militia, then walked off in the direction of the smithy.

Everyone was silent for a long moment after Shadrack and the men left. Jem wondered if things were really that bad. What it would happen if the food stores ran out?

Whooo, whooo, whooo, Omen called.

"That's the puzzle, birdlet," Phaedra said. "Who, who, who gonna be the next to go? And will it be by English bullet or empty belly?"

Jem was only half listening. Still thinking about what Big Sunday had said, he turned to stare at the spot where Omen perched on the watchtower beam surveying the yard as though it were his princely domain.

Their gazes met and held for a moment. What manner of secrets hid behind those fierce yellow eyes?

And then, with brief squawk that said, *wouldn't you like to know*, Omen lifted his wings and sailed off.

Chapter Twenty-Two

May 12, 1740

Jem got part of the answer to his question about Omen a few mornings later while he was clearing the smudge pits.

He should've been fishing, but the last three times he'd come back with an empty string. It was as though the fish could smell how hungry he was, and kept well away. Phaedra had accused him of loafing, and she had come up with a host of chores to keep him busy.

As he swept, a long ash separated itself from the rest and swirled above his broom before coming to rest at his feet. His breath caught as he stooped to examine what appeared to be the remains of a thin black feather. But when he touched it, it disintegrated. A sign of flight? Would someone else be leaving?

"Look what I found," Maribel said.

At the sound of her voice, Jem dropped the broom. A cloud of ashes filled the air. When he glanced up, he saw that she held Shadrack's conjure bag by the hide strap.

"Don't surprise a body like that!" he said. "Let me see that. Where'd you find it?"

"Along the trail," she said, handing it to him. "What is it?"

The pouch was pulled open, its contents gone. What had happened to the charm? He hesitated. Best not speak to her of conjure; it might get back to the general or the priests. Besides, an idea was starting to take shape in the back of his head.

"It's a kind of carrying pouch. For small things."

"What kind of things?"

"Little things, like beads and berries."

"I shall put orange blossoms and lace in it and give it to Phaedra."

Jem marveled at how Maribel's English had improved. "Why do you want to do that?" he asked.

"As a present. So she will know I am her friend."

"Whyever would you want to be friends with Phaedra? She hates everyone."

"She does not. She is sad, like I was when Mama died."

Jem frowned. Phaedra was many things. Spiteful, bossy, contrary, and argumentative, just to name a few. But he had never thought of her as sad.

"I like Phaedra," Maribel said.

Jem squinted at her. *Were they talking about the same woman?* "What's there to like about her?"

"She is clever," Maribel said. "She weaves baskets and makes good stew from almost anything."

Phaedra, clever? But when he studied on it, Jem had to admit that there was a sort of deviousness about her. Hadn't she gotten away with saying and doing things that had the rest of them shaking their heads?

"Phaedra wouldn't like it." Jem sniffed. "It smells foul. Leave it with me to bury and I'll whittle you a pretty bird to give her. If there's one thing Phaedra likes, it's birds."

Maribel considered the idea for a moment. "*Un bonito pájaro*," she said. "A pretty bird." She handed him the bag. "But not an owl," she added. "Owls scare me."

As she walked away, Jem put the bag around his neck and concealed it under his shirt, making sure the strap didn't show. It didn't sit right with him, wearing Shadrack's empty charm, but he was fair certain Omen had taken it and swallowed the contents. Jem felt badly about the worry its loss had caused the old man.

If Omen had eaten the charm, it was only a matter of time before whatever was left of it came back up.

Finding the pellets wasn't so easy now that Omen was flying. As he swept the yard the next morning, Jem watched the owl. He checked several times under Omen's various perches, but there was no pellet. Still, he was convinced that Omen was the thief.

Jem was determined to make things right for old Shadrack. He thought back to the herbs Aunt Winnie dried on the kitchen rafters, and the little pots of bones, ashes, and graveyard dust she always hid in the cellar. Countless times he'd watched her mix charms. He could do it! He'd make a charm to replace the one Omen stole.

Jem got the collection from under his bed and took it outside. He selected the best of the small bones to go into the bag.

Omen flew down to investigate. He strutted and craned his neck as he inspected.

"Keep away," Jem told the owl when he tried for the third time to stick his beak into the bag. "It's your wrong I'm trying to right."

Omen stalked off, then flew low several times around the yard, only to land on the drying rack and make a mess of the grass.

"I'm sorry I was cross with you."

Omen flew back to his perch and glared at him. Jem didn't have time to make up with the sulky owl. He placed the bones in the pouch along with some ashes from the fire.

He put the conjure bag in his pocket and was walking back to the chosa with his collection of skeletons when he realized what he'd left out.

Chapter Twenty-Three

May 14, 1740

A mighty wind stirred the palm fronds on the roof. Jem heard Omen's call and went outside to check on him.

There was something Jem needed from Omen, but he wasn't sure how to get it. In the early light, he could see the owl perched on the watchtower, gripping a dark mass in his talons and tearing at it with his beak. His feather horns fluttered in the wind, but the platform above protected him from the stronger gusts. Omen looked up from his catch as Jem approached.

Dark leaves swirled in the dirt beneath the tower. Only they weren't leaves, Jem saw as he got closer. They were feathers. Black feathers.

Omen had killed a crow.

Jem wasn't certain whether the tight feeling in his chest was pride or revulsion. He waited at the corner of the tower for Omen to finish his meal, willing him to hurry so he could clean up before Phaedra noticed. Last thing he needed was Omen proving her right about being a predator to the crows; she'd start in about her chickens again. Also, he needed a feather. One of Omen's wing feathers. Reynard had said they were valuable to the tribes up north. That must mean they held powerful magic. The way Jem saw it, Omen owed Shadrack a bit of his magic to repay him for stealing his charm. He needed to distract Omen.

"Did I tell you how Brother Rabbit got Bear's tooth for the Sky God?" Jem called out.

The owl paid no attention.

"No? Well now, it's a good tale all right. Better come down here to listen to it." Jem spoke loud enough to be heard over the roar of the wind.

Brother Rabbit was always trying to pull one over on Brother Bear. He knew that the old critter was mighty greedy and that his favorite food was honey. Whenever Bear smelled honey, he wouldn't rest until he'd found it and eaten it all. One day Brother Rabbit found a hive in the middle of a split tree. He got a hard stick of oak and covered it with honey.

Before long, Bear came lumbering along, sniffing the air.

"This is your lucky day," Brother Rabbit said. "If you'll guard this hive while I find a pot, I'll share the honey with you."

"I'll do it," Bear said, his big mouth watering.

Now, Brother Rabbit knew Bear would be into that honey soon as his back was turned, but he scampered out of sight.

Bear could have climbed up and taken the honey from the hive. But he was lazy. When he saw the stick covered with honey, he thought it was a piece of honeycomb Brother Rabbit had taken from the hive. Bear was happy to have Brother Rabbit do all the work for him. He tossed the stick into the air, caught it in his mouth, and took a big chomp.

Can you guess what happened next?

The trees shook with Bear's roar of pain. He staggered around the clearing and bumped right into the split tree. The hive toppled out and those bees were powerful wrathy.

They chased Bear through the forest for so long, he may be running still. But he left something behind.

When Brother Rabbit came back, he laughed and laughed. There on the ground was the honey-covered stick with one of Bear's sharpest teeth stuck in it.

Whaaa, whaaa! Omen made his after-meal call.

Jem looked up in time to see him drop what was left of the carcass. He swept up the remains and buried them with the ashes from last night's fire. But before he shoveled dirt over what was left of the crow, he retrieved a few of the glossy black feathers. The touch of them made him shiver, but he was sure that along with Omen's feather, they were just what he needed for the charm bag.

Only Omen wasn't inclined to give up one of his feathers.

"Come down," Jem said. "It'll only take a moment."

The owl ignored him, grooming his talons with his beak. So Jem climbed up the ladder to his perch. *Best do this quickly,* he decided. He'd brought a salamander as an offering, but Omen was full. He turned his head away.

"You won't even notice this." Taking advantage of Omen's disinterest, Jem seized one of the smaller of his lower wing feathers and jerked it out.

Screeeeech! Omen turned on Jem in a flash and nipped his finger.

"Owww!" Jem cried. "You drew blood!"

Omen glared at him and snapped his beak, his feather horns rising.

"I didn't mean to hurt you!" Jem put a hand out to stroke the owl's head.

Omen snapped again and made a barking call.

Jem backed down the ladder slowly. "I'm sorry," he said. The owl had shed so many baby feathers, it hadn't occurred to him that taking one would hurt. First he'd pushed him out of a tree, now he'd plucked him. He couldn't blame Omen for not trusting him. "I'll make it up to you," Jem promised.

Omen lifted his wings and flew off.

⚊ ⁓ ⚊

Omen still hadn't forgiven him the next afternoon. Jem tried everything he knew, but the owl wouldn't let him get close. It was going to take a while to make things right with Omen. He best settle with Shadrack first. So he volunteered to fetch a load of sweetgrass for Phaedra. Luckily even though her baskets weren't selling anymore, she hadn't stopped making them.

"Go on, then." She eyed him suspiciously. "But hurry back."

Jem had worked out a plan. He'd tell Shadrack he had come by to ask when the next load of charcoal would be ready, then he'd pretend to find the conjure bag on the ground.

Instead of heading east toward the marsh, he took the trail west. As he left it and entered the trees, Jem gripped the charmed beads on his shirt with one hand, his knife with the other. It was harder to find Shadrack's place than he'd imagined. As long as he smelled the pine and myrtle, he knew he wasn't close. Pine had too much resin to make good charcoal. Jem walked past the tall trees to the oak and hickory forest beyond.

It was here that Shadrack had built his kiln, right in the middle of the forest, so logs could be dragged from all directions. Jem eventually found the clearing. The first clue was the light coming from an opening in the tree cover. Then he spotted the tree trunks jutting out from the ground, and the piles of logs and brush ringing the outer edges.

The signs of habitation comforted Jem. He felt somehow lighter, being back in the forest. Maybe it was relief at the thought of making up for what Omen had done, but as he made his way to the kiln, sparrow song and the smell of sassafras made him feel like his old self, before the attack that night in the woods, before the war and hunger started.

At first he couldn't see Shadrack's chosa. It was nestled so snugly against a group of trees that he almost missed it. It sagged between two elms, seemingly held together only by a blanket of vines. The kiln itself was round and low, wider than a chosa, and covered with mud. A finger of smoke rose from its center.

Jem called out as he approached, but there was no answer.

The door was a hide flap outlined in a watery blue stain, a conjure charm to keep evil from entering. A shiver traveled up Jem's spine, and he felt the familiar sensation of eyes on him. Was the charm he made powerful enough to work? He searched the tree trunks for signs of movement. When he'd been a child in Charles Town, the line between good and evil had been sharp and clear. Here in Spanish Florida, it seemed to be drawn in shifting sands. Sometimes it was difficult to tell right from wrong, friend from foe.

"Shadrack?"

No answer.

He started to peek inside the hut, but held back. Already he'd broken Omen's trust by stealing his feather, and now he was set to deceive Shadrack with a replacement conjure charm. He'd not add to the weight of these sins by sneaking into Shadrack's quarters as well.

Then he spied a nail hammered into a plank beside the doorway. This must be the place Shadrack had mentioned. Jem took the conjure bag from his pocket and wrapped the string three times around the nail.

Snap.

Jem froze. Shadrack had caught him in the act. Jem's heart pounded as he thought of what to say, settling on telling Shadrack he'd found the bag in the woods.

"Was just bringing—" He turned to face the old man.

No one was there.

The clearing was empty, and the sparrows had stopped singing.

"Domingo?"

Taking a step back, Jem tripped on a vine and almost fell. He hadn't noticed the long reach of the spindly tendrils. It wasn't just the chosa they covered, but the trees on either side. The vines were a blanket of grasping fingers, reaching out for him.

With a quick look back at the conjure bag swaying on the nail, Jem ran.

"Where's my grass?" Phaedra demanded as Jem entered the fort.

"There's something out there," he panted.

"Where?" she said.

"By Shadrack's place."

"You were supposed to be at the marsh."

Jem tried to think fast. "Reckoned I'd dig some palm roots first."

"Without a basket?"

General Rojas strutted over. "Did you see something, boy?"

"Just like the night I was attacked, there's something out there!"

"Likely the young fool caught sight of the old fool moving around out there in the woods," Phaedra said. "The boy's trying to lie himself out of trouble."

"It wasn't Shadrack," Jem said. "It was someone, something else!"

"I shall send a scouting party," the general said.

"No need," Big Sunday said. "Probably just an animal."

"Boy's prone to skittishness," Phaedra added. "Scared by his own shadow."

Jem left them and walked toward the watchtower. Big Sunday's doubt seeped through his veins like cold water. He wasn't surprised that Phaedra and Rojas distrusted him, but Big Sunday's betrayal stung.

"If you're looking for that owl," Phaedra called, "he's gone."

"What do you mean? I just saw him this morning." Jem could still see Omen glaring at him, yellow eyes injured and accusing. He'd have to hunt hard for victuals to make up for what he'd done. "Did he fly over the north wall?"

"Didn't fly. That bird ran like the old trickster he is. This time I believe I chased him off once and for all."

"What'd you do?" Jem said, his voice rising. "You didn't hurt him, did you?"

"Not as much as I should have liked to. But I will if he comes back."

Jem's temples throbbed. "What happened?" Omen was already upset by what Jem had done to him; he would have been in bad humor.

Phaedra glared at him. "That demon with wings landed up on the chicken coop and hissed at me. I got my broom and fetched him off. It's governor's orders to save every bit we have. Can't have that owl killing chickens."

The muscles in Jem's neck relaxed slightly. "Where'd he go?"

"Ran up over the west wall, trying to fool me with that wing trick."

Jem turned and headed to the gate.

"Where do you think you're going? You've chores—"

Jem didn't wait to hear any more. He ran out of the fort and started up the trail to the forest. All he cared about was finding Omen. It was wrong that he stole the feather. He could see that now. It didn't matter that he was trying to make up for something Omen had done. He didn't even know for sure it was Omen that took the charm in the first place. He'd broken his promise to himself to take care of Omen. And for what? To make a charm he didn't even know would work?

"Why the hurry, my young friend?" Reynard called from the trail.

Relieved to see the trader, Jem hurried to catch up to him. "Have you seen Omen?"

"Can't say as I have." Reynard took off his possum cap and mopped his brow. "Is he lost?"

Jem scanned the tree line as he spoke. "Phaedra went at him with the broom and I think he's hurt."

"Why'd she do that?"

"Said it was on account of he landed on the chicken coop. She thought he was after one of the chickens and we need all we got on account of we only have enough food for a month."

"A month?" Reynard said. "That's not much. Is that really all you have?"

"Probably," Jem said. "That's what the governor says, anyway. Holler if you see him, will you? You headed north?"

"Just trying to keep ahead of any trouble." Reynard tipped his cap and whistled to Celeste. "I'll call out if I see your owl."

Jem started toward the woods. He felt the old dread when he got there, but near the edge, he saw a small grove of poplars. He searched out the tallest one. It was tricky to get up on that first limb, but once there he had no trouble climbing onto the higher branches. He stopped in a place that had a good view over the surrounding area.

Looking down made him feel a bit queasy, so he lifted his eyes and concentrated on the treetops.

An egret flew past, then a couple of sparrows. But no Omen.

He took up his owl whistle and blew.

There was no answering call.

Jem found he liked being aloft. The needles on the nearby pines smelled clean. The limbs of the poplar felt solid and strong. He gazed out at the treetops, listening for Omen's call.

He dared to look down again. Somehow, it didn't seem as frightful this time. Mose's earthen walls appeared small and insignificant from up so high. People scurried around the yard like beetles. The well was a small basket and some of the chosas seemed to lean like makeshift toys.

He gazed up at the afternoon sky. A heavy band of clouds parted, revealing a patch of deep blue. If only he could fly. He and Omen could sail off, far out of reach of Phaedra and her broom. It must be the most wonderful feeling to leave the hard earth behind and soar above the trees.

When he called through the owl whistle again, it seemed all living things in the forest—birds, squirrels, insects, even the trees themselves—stilled, as though they, too, waited for an answer.

He heard a noise from below. A drum? No.

Hoofbeats.

He peered over at the trail leading in from the north. Nothing. He was about to turn away when, out of the corner of his eye, he saw movement.

Coming toward Mose, about a mile away, was a group of four men on horseback.

The barrels of their muskets glinted in the afternoon sun. He recognized the red uniforms from the streets of Charles Town.

English scouts!

Chapter Twenty-Four

May 15, 1740

Jem's breath came fast and heavy. He skinned his palms
and twice nearly lost his grip clambering down the tree.

After all this time, they'd finally come. And he was the
one to spy them! He must go back and warn the people of
Mose!

Reaching the lowest branch, he dropped to the ground.
He ignored the pain in his feet and started off through the
forest.

He opened his mouth to cry out when he reached the
field within sight of the fort's walls, but decided to keep
quiet. The English might hear him and know they'd been
spotted.

He bounded up to the gate.

"What's the hurry?" Juba said. "Looks like you seen a
spirit."

"English!" Jem gasped. "Coming south…just off the trail!"

Juba waved to Big Sunday and General Rojas and they hurried over. "Boy says he's seen English."

Big Sunday peered down at him gravely. "What did you see?"

Rojas stepped in front of him. "Tell us," he ordered.

"Four...four of them on horseback," Jem said, still panting. "Over by the creek."

"How'd you see them if they're not visible from the watchtower?" Big Sunday asked.

"And how do you know they didn't see you?" Rojas demanded.

"I was up a tree."

The general glared at Jem, his lip curling in a sneer.

"It's the English, I swear it!" Jem cried.

Big Sunday studied him for a moment longer. "I believe him."

Rojas frowned. "You will be held accountable if the boy is lying."

Big Sunday nodded. "Don't ring the bell." He started toward the watchtower, but Rojas pushed past him and climbed halfway up the ladder. "We must all go to the Castillo de San Marcos," he called. "Governor's standing orders."

Jem stopped in his tracks. Weren't they going to stay and fight? It never occurred to him that they'd just give up. It was four scouts he saw, not the whole English army. Still, he remembered how small Mose looked from above. All around him was frenzied motion, cries and shouts filling the yard with sound.

Phaedra grabbed him by the shoulders. "You heard him, move!"

"But aren't we going to—"Jem didn't have a chance to finish his question.

People were already tossing possessions out of chosas.

Phaedra started rolling blankets. "Help me get these loaded," she ordered.

"We can't abandon the fort," he said. "It's our home!"

"Some home!" Phaedra said. "But it don't matter. Governor's orders."

As much as Jem wanted to stay and fight, the thought of finally going to the Castillo was exciting. Then he had another thought. "I can't leave now," he said. "Not till I find Omen."

"He's flown far away if he has any sense."

"If his wing is broken, he won't be able to fly."

"If his wing is broken, there's nothing you can do for him."

Jem stared at her.

"What did you think?" Phaedra said. "That you'd march into the Castillo de San Marcos with that bird on your shoulder?" She shook her head. "I can see it now. Owl flying hither and yon, terrorizing the horses and dropping cow dung in the cook pots." She shook her head. "You'd have us handed over to the English, every last one of us."

Jem's chest tightened. He'd made a promise. "I'll just make sure he's all right. Then I'll run to the Castillo."

She ignored this. "Help me gather the cutlery. Use this basket."

Jem kept an eye on his climbing wall. When no one was looking, he'd be gone in a trice. He bided his time, waiting for his chance.

But Phaedra didn't let him get more than three feet from her.

"I'll check with Big Sunday about what to load next," he told her.

"You'll do no such thing." She grabbed his sleeve. "Don't think I can't see the truth of what you're planning, just like that night you run off into the woods."

He shook her hand off. "You don't know anything about me!"

"I know you're a sorry liar. Don't take up cards."

"You hate me. Why not let me go?" Jem blinked at her furiously.

"I don't have the time or inclination to go chasing after you, and I keep my promises."

"But you said yourself the oath wasn't binding!"

"Don't sass," she snapped. "Chickens need fetching. Gather them up and put them in these." She thrust two lidded baskets at him.

Big Sunday appeared in the doorway of the chosa, a musket in his hands.

"I need to find Omen," Jem told him.

Big Sunday shook his head. "This is no child's game. The governor's orders are that at the first sign of the English, everyone goes to the Castillo. No one stays behind."

"What about Domingo?" Jem's voice trembled. "Does he have to go?"

"Don't worry about him." Big Sunday's face was calm.

"It isn't fair that some of us have to follow orders and others don't." Jem tried to keep the quiver out of his voice, but he felt breathless and his throat ached.

"You will help pack the wagons and go to the Castillo without any further sass. If you disobey, I will take you over my knee."

"Amen to that," Phaedra cried.

"Hush," Sunday told her and turned back to Jem. "Understand?"

Over the noise of confused animals and the din of people chattering, Jem heard his own voice, now steady.

"Yes sir."

Chapter Twenty-Five

May 15, 1740

The line of people who had fled Mose snaked around the western wall to where the lowered drawbridge extended over the moat, providing the only way in or out of the Castillo de San Marcos. Guards were searching every basket and pack.

"The English'll be upon us, and those fools will still be pawing through our personal effects," Phaedra said. "The general told us we were only allowed one small pack each. Just look at how much some people brought." Jem thought it best not to mention the large baskets Phaedra had ordered him to lug all the way from the fort.

There'd been no sign of Domingo as they passed through the Indian village. When Jem glimpsed the worry in Big Sunday's expression, he felt ashamed about what he'd said.

He kept his eyes turned toward Mose, hoping to see Omen. And what about Reynard? The trader was clever enough to make it out ahead of the scouts; Jem was sure of it.

"Look there," Jem said, pointing out the thin wisp of

smoke that rose from the woods. Had anyone told Shadrack that the English were coming?

"Don't it just figure," Phaedra said. "That old simpleton fires a load of charcoal just in time for the enemy to forge their blades with it."

"I'll run back and warn him!" Jem started in the direction of the smoke.

Phaedra grabbed his arm. "You're not going anywhere. Governor's orders."

The line was moving more quickly now. Phaedra pushed him along in front of her. As they neared the entrance to the Castillo, Jem spied a mound of cast-off belongings.

One of the guards took a spinning wheel from a woman and tossed it onto the pile. It balanced precariously for a moment before rolling off and plunging onto the hard ground of the dry moat where cows, pigs, and sheep grazed. Although the Castillo was large compared to Mose, its walls held only rooms where supplies, weapons, and soldiers would be housed. The people would camp in the open-air area surrounded by the castle walls. The yard was about half the size of a cornfield.

Jem was glad he hadn't tried to bring his collection. He'd wrapped Omen's baby feathers in a palm leaf and tucked the bundle into his pocket. The bones and snake rattle were hidden under a pile of hay in the coop back at Mose.

The guard released Phaedra's chickens into the moat. All the livestock would be kept there, protected by banks of earth rising above, yet still reachable from inside the Castillo.

"We'll never see them again," Phaedra said as they scattered. "That's a good laying hen," she called. "Don't you go roasting her!"

The soldier ignored Phaedra and waved them on. They crossed the drawbridge and passed through a heavy paneled door. Jem touched the stone walls. "Must be at least fifteen feet thick," he whispered.

"Move along," Phaedra said.

Jem swallowed. Ever since he'd first seen St. Augustine, he'd dreamed of entering the Castillo de San Marcos. Now that he was finally here, he hesitated. The smell of tobacco smoke and the harsh sound of men's laughter took him back to his old life in Charles Town.

The walls of the Castillo were thick, the air heavy and musty. The towering stone archway closed in, threatening to squeeze the breath out of him. Jem fought to remember where he was.

It took a hard push from Phaedra to propel him into the dark hallway.

Through the open door to one room, he glimpsed bunks lining the walls. In another, a group of soldiers sat at one end of a rough-hewn table, playing cards. The room stank of sweat and stale cigar smoke, but their voices, speaking Spanish, didn't sound threatening.

Phaedra yanked Jem back by the collar. He must have stepped too close to the door. She glared but said nothing. Shoving him in front of her, she followed close on his heels down the passage.

All at once, they were cast out into the sunlight and heat

of the courtyard in the center of the Castillo. Door and window openings were cut into the stone walls, which rose two stories all around them like a square casket. Over these were the gun decks and bastions where the cannons were mounted.

The courtyard was already crowded. Black-gowned Spanish matrons presided over stacks of possessions while children played tag among the rows of hastily built campsites. The women acknowledged the people from Mose with grim nods. The yard was smaller than Jem had imagined. Or maybe it seemed that way because it was so crowded. A cook fire added heat and smoke to the hum of voices that filled the air. It was like market day in the St. Augustine plaza, but it had a different feel. Voices were low and urgent, faces closed and pinched with worry.

"There." Phaedra pointed to a spot where some others from Mose had gathered, and they headed over to join them.

Jem dropped the bundles and helped Phaedra stack them. It didn't take long. The blankets, some eating utensils, a few articles of clothing, and basket makings were all they had.

Phaedra went to help with the cooking. "You watch our things," she said.

He nodded, but as soon as her back was turned, he headed off in the opposite direction to prowl the courtyard. There were too many people about to see much more than the ground beneath his feet.

People clustered around a doorway. The acrid smell of incense and the hushed murmur of prayers came from within. A black-robed priest stood at an altar before crowded benches. Dust motes danced in the lone beam of sunlight that shone through an opening high up on the opposite wall.

Jem walked on. Most of the other rooms held supplies: food in one space, cannonballs and weapons in another. Spanish soldiers presided over each—counting, stacking, and organizing everything into piles and barrels.

Three wells were spaced around the courtyard. Soldiers hoisted water in oaken buckets and passed them out to lines of waiting citizens.

More soldiers stood guard outside a closed door. Jem reckoned it was the governor's quarters.

Not far from the door, he caught sight of Big Sunday and the general. He tried to get closer, but the crowd was too thick. The press of people carried him along.

He squinted up at the gun deck. From there, the soldiers had a view of the harbor, the town, and all the way back to Mose. Jem longed to venture up the stairs to the top. Maybe he could see Omen. But only the militia and soldiers were allowed.

"Phaedra's looking for you."

Jem whirled around. It was Maribel. Flustered at her sudden appearance, he could barely think what to say. "T-tell her you couldn't find me," he stuttered.

She gazed at him skeptically and he realized the excuse wouldn't work in such close quarters. Phaedra would likely start calling for him and kick up a fuss. He'd have to bide his time while he figured out what to do about Omen. "All right," he sighed, and followed Maribel through the crowd to the cook fire.

At first, the excitement of being in the Castillo made time fly. Jem spent hours watching the soldiers, the Spanish officials, and the Mose militia up on the gun deck. He enjoyed living among the Spanish and trying to understand their language.

But soon the newness wore off. The days fell into a similar pattern: watered porridge for breakfast and watered stew for dinner. Between mealtimes, Jem tried to avoid Phaedra, but she always managed to find him and set him to some tiresome task. There was no place to hide—no forest to escape to. He even grew tired of watching the people in the yard. They had become irritable and quarrelsome in the cramped quarters. The only peace he got was in the evenings when he sat and carved atlatls.

"Why don't you go back to carving whistles?" Phaedra said. "Soldiers are just gonna take those spear throwers and burn them for fuel once the wood piles get low."

Working on the atlatls kept Jem's thoughts on Domingo. Where was he now? Would his atlatl and spear keep him safe from the English? No matter what Phaedra said, Jem was determined to continue his whittling. It helped him focus on a future outside the walls of the Castillo, a future where he could fend for himself. Jem prayed Omen wasn't too badly injured to do the same. If only he could get out and find him.

It was getting late. Jem put his atlatls away. The heat

made it hard to go to sleep. And when he finally drifted off, the dreams came.

It was after midnight. Master and his friends were playing cards. Jem was supposed to be waiting on them but must have nodded off. He awoke to a slap.

"Fetch my snuff pouch," Master ordered.

Jem, only five or six years old, forgot Aunt Winnie's warnings not to speak and to come to her if he didn't understand what Master wanted.

"Snuff?" he repeated stupidly.

Master's eyes went wide, and Jem got scared. But then Master smiled. "Hear that?" he'd said to his friends. "Boy doesn't know about snuff. Perhaps I should show him?" Master opened a small silver box and crooked his finger. "Open your mouth," he said and stuffed some dark leaves in Jem's mouth.

Jem chewed them carefully. He knew all about the curative powers of leaves and bark. Aunt Winnie gave him sassafras to chew when his belly ached. But the leaves from Master's box had a bitter, sour taste. He swallowed them quickly.

"Don't worry about the snuff pouch," Master said in a surprisingly gentle voice. "You just go over there to the corner and I'll call if I need something."

Jem did as he was told. But he couldn't understand why the other men were watching him so carefully. He smiled so they'd think he liked the snuff. He'd tell Aunt Winnie that she should give Master some of her leaves, which tasted better.

After a few minutes, Jem began to feel sick.

"Your boy is turning green," one of the men said.

"Serves him right," Master replied. "Next time I ask for snuff, I expect he'll know what I mean. Retch on my carpet and I'll beat your hide," he called over his shoulder to Jem.

So he stood in the corner, breathing their smoke and choking on his bile while the men laughed and laughed.

Jem woke with a start, the cruel laughter ringing in his ears.

Nightmares ruined his sleep, and Phaedra hounded his waking hours. It had been hard to get away from her at Fort Mose; here it was impossible.

A few nights later some of the people from Mose huddled in a cramped corner of the yard. It was too hot for a fire. Big Sunday had finished his watch on the gun deck and come down to visit. He looked exhausted.

"Are they still out there?" Jem asked. The Castillo yard felt like a deep hole they couldn't see out of.

"Who?"

"The English."

"They're not going anywhere," Big Sunday snapped. Then he rubbed his eyes and gave Jem a weary smile. "Sorry, the waiting is wearing on all of us. And I miss Mose."

Jem missed it, too. "Will you tell us a story?" He was almost afraid to ask.

The captain smiled. "Been bad down here with Phaedra?"
He shrugged.

"I ever told you folks the one about the frog and the mouse?" Sunday asked the group.

"Tell it," Adine said.

"A while back, there was a frog and a mouse who were good friends. They didn't live in the same place, though. The mouse lived in a hole in the ground and the frog lived in the water. The mouse couldn't go in the water. So when they wanted to visit, the frog would come out of his pond. When the visit was over, the frog would jump back into the water and the mouse would go back into his hole."

Jem loved hearing Big Sunday tell stories. He admired the way he drew his listeners in as he talked.

"But one day," Big Sunday went on, "when the frog came out to visit, he got a wicked notion in his heart. He took some string and tied his foot and the mouse's foot together. Then the frog jumped back into the pond, taking the mouse with him.

"Now the mouse, as you know, couldn't live in water. Soon he died. After a while, the mouse got all swole up and floated to the surface of the pond.

"Round about that time, a hawk flew by and spied him. That old hawk swooped down and took both the dead mouse and the live frog up to his nest in the treetops."

"How'd the frog escape?" Jem asked.

Big Sunday shook his head. "Hawk ate them both."

Jem didn't need to ask what the story meant. He was tied

to Phaedra sure as the mouse was tied to the frog. They were in a hole, all right. When he glanced around the circle, he caught Phaedra glaring at him.

One of the militiamen came over and whispered in Big Sunday's ear. The captain's eyes widened. Then he rose and departed without a word.

Chapter Twenty-Six

May 29, 1740

W here do you think you're going?" Phaedra asked. "Privy," Jem replied, trying to sound innocent. He took a few more strides, and when he knew Phaedra could no longer see him, he turned and headed in the direction Big Sunday had gone.

Jem saw him speak to a soldier and pass through the arch that led to the covered way, but when he tried to follow, the soldier blocked his path. Jem walked on and waited. In a few minutes Big Sunday strode back through the door. But he wasn't alone. Domingo was by his side!

Jem started to call out, but the expressions on their faces stopped him. Something was wrong.

They were so deep in conversation that they didn't notice Jem behind them. He tried to catch what they were saying, but they spoke in Domingo's language.

Jem stepped back out of sight when they stopped in front of the large door that led to the governor's office. Big Sunday spoke to the guard and he and Domingo were allowed to enter. Through the open door, Jem could see the governor and the commander of the Castillo rising from their chairs.

"My son brings news," Big Sunday said.

Jem edged closer. When the guard looked at him suspiciously, he crouched and pretended to search for something on the ground. But he had no trouble overhearing the captain's words to the governor. "The English are occupying Fort Mose."

Stunned, Jem stared hard at the packed earth at his feet. A fragment of oyster shell was embedded there, a tiny bit of blue showing in its white surface. Taken? What did Big Sunday mean? The English couldn't take Mose. It wasn't theirs! Why were they always trying to take what didn't belong to them?

Before he could hear more, the door closed. Jem made his way back to the others, his chest heavy, eyes stinging.

In the June heat, the courtyard was as hot as Shadrack's kiln. People jostled and pushed to get into the shaded areas, which shifted as the sun cut a blazing path across the sky. The group from Mose sat in a circle, fanning themselves with palm leaves. Jem joined them, head down, unable to look at anyone. Instead he took up the atlatl he'd been working on and kept his eyes on it. He felt as small and powerless as he had back in Charles Town.

Soon Big Sunday returned and told them the news.

"We should've stayed and fought for Mose," Juba said. "Instead of letting ourselves be crowded in here like livestock."

"We'd all be on our way back to Carolina if we'd stayed out there," Phaedra said. "That, or dead. You think the Mose militia could've fought off the English by itself?"

"Governor could have sent soldiers," Adine said. "Rooster General always going on about how they the best fighters in all of Christendom."

"Why would the Spanish risk their hides for us?" Phaedra asked.

Jem wanted to shout at her, but decided he couldn't risk a fight. Besides, he didn't have the strength. The usual allotment of stew and hard biscuit was barely enough to keep him going; now even those were running low. Jem hadn't had anything to eat since last evening.

⬤ ⬤

As the sun sank below the Castillo walls, Jem thought about how Aunt Winnie had told him that dusk was a magic time. Anything could happen, she said, in that moment between the two worlds of day and night.

"Look!" someone cried.

Jem glanced up in time to see an owl fly over the Castillo.

He could hardly believe it. Not only was Omen unhurt, he'd been looking for Jem—and now he had found him. His eyes swam. He'd never seen anything so beautiful, so majestic. He waved and shouted, "I'm here, Omen!"

As his gaze followed the owl's flight, something else caught his eye. On the gun deck above, a musket barrel pointed to the heavens.

He gasped. "Noooooo!" But it was too late.

Crack! The sound of the shot echoed once and the yard went silent.

The owl lurched, then dropped from the sky.

Jem rushed past people, jumping over barrels and bedrolls.

"*Alto!* Stop!" Someone grabbed his arm. Jem twisted free and ran.

He dropped to his knees beside the fallen owl. The musket ball had ripped through its breast feathers. Its talons quivered as blood pooled on the packed earth.

Jem gagged. He couldn't make sense of what he was seeing. Resting his forehead in his hands, he tried to catch his breath.

It wasn't Omen.

Relief washed over him. He gazed up at the sky. "Thank you," he whispered to the Sky God.

"*Loco.*" A rough hand pulled him up. It was the soldier from the gun deck, still holding his musket.

Jem backed away. It may not have been Omen, but an owl had still been shot. "Don't you know it's bad luck to kill an owl?" he shouted.

The soldier's frown communicated scorn as well as any words. "*Que?*"

"*Estupido,*" another man said. "We need eat, no?"

The soldier with the gun pushed Jem. "Go!"

Jem took one more look at the owl before he turned and made his way back to the group from Mose.

"Sorry about your pet," Juba said.

"It wasn't Omen." Jem didn't want to talk, so he got his knife and the atlatl he was working on and sat down next to Domingo. Since bringing the news about Mose, Domingo had stayed at the Castillo. Jem wanted to tell him how relieved he'd been to see that he was all right, but that feeling was tangled up in a web of guilt and sorrow.

Whoo, whoo, whoo!

Jem put down his knife. Had he imagined the call? Could it have been the spirit of the dead owl calling out for vengeance?

Domingo must have heard it too, for he stood up and squinted into the gathering darkness.

Phaedra called from the cook fire, "Go and fetch some water."

Jem ignored her.

The owl hooted again.

Now Phaedra stood over him, holding the water bucket. "You hear me?"

Again, the owl called.

"What does it mean?" Jem fought the urge to cover his ears against the mournful sound.

"Dead one's mate calls to him," Domingo said. "Owls have only one."

A strange expression came over Phaedra's face.

"What'll happen to her?" Jem asked.

"She'll likely die."

"I'll get the water myself," Phaedra said, wiping something out of the corner of her eye. Could it be that she was sorry for the owl? Jem studied on it for a moment. No. If Phaedra was sorry, it was for herself.

"Look!" someone shouted. Jem shut his eyes. He couldn't bear to see another owl drop out of the sky.

Footsteps pounded on the gun deck.

A call carried over the yard of the Castillo, first in Spanish, then in English. "Ships! Ships in the mouth of the harbor!"

Chapter Twenty-Seven

June 14, 1740

Why doesn't the commander fire the cannons?" Adine asked. "He's let the English sail into the harbor where they're right on top of us."

"Commander wants them to get in position to fire first," Big Sunday said. "He's waiting until their ships and cannons are in range. Then we'll have a chance of trapping them in the crossfire between the bastions."

"But won't their cannons also be able to fire on us if they get much closer?" she asked.

"That's right. But there's only so much powder and ammunition, so we'll have to take that chance." Big Sunday looked tired. He'd just come down from the gun deck after a long time on duty. "It is risky. With the English blocking the harbor, no ships from Spain or Cuba can reach us. But what choice do we have?"

Jem saw the worry in Big Sunday's eyes. How long could they hold out without supplies or reinforcements? Without food? There had to be a solution. His stomach rumbled. "You gonna eat the rest of that?" he asked, pointing to Phaedra's bowl.

"Isn't fit for hogs." She turned back to the basket she was sewing. Why she kept making them, Jem didn't know. There was no call for baskets now. "You can have it."

Jem didn't care. He finished the watery stew in three gulps and licked the bowl.

A shout came from the gun deck. *"Atención!"*

"I've got to get back," Big Sunday said. "Get down, all of you!"

There were more shouts in Spanish, then the scrambling of feet. Flashes of red and blue crossed the gun deck as soldiers ran to their posts.

"They're in position," one of the men from Mose called down. "Ready!"

Jem ducked as they'd been told to do, still clutching the empty bowl.

"Valor!" A voice rang out. "Courage!"

As if in reply, English cannon fire boomed.

The governor stood above them on the gun deck, facing the crowd below, the morning sunlight glinting off the gold buttons on his coat.

The ground shook, but there was no explosion. Jem figured that the lead balls had missed the Castillo wall.

The governor stumbled, almost pitching into the courtyard. He turned back toward the harbor, the silk-tasseled epaulets on his uniform swaying, and crossed himself as he regained his balance. Turning back to the commander of the Castillo on the gun deck, he raised a fist in the air.

"Fuego!" the commander ordered.

The Spanish cannons roared their response.

Jem rolled into a ball and curled his arms up around his head. He thought of the thunder Brother Rabbit used to draw Snake out of his den. Cannon fire was much louder when you were right below it, not two miles away. Smoke from burning powder filled the yard. Nearby, a baby cried. He closed his eyes tight and hugged his knees to his chest.

BOOM! BOOM! BOOM! Several explosions sounded across the harbor. The ground trembled and Jem heard a mighty splash coming from near the eastern wall.

He clenched his teeth so tight his head ached. When he opened his eyes, Phaedra was staring at him. "I never should have brought you here," she said. "We're all gonna die."

Jem edged closer to her. He was grateful to be near anyone at that moment, even Phaedra. He thought about what she'd just said. Was she actually admitting she'd been wrong? "Why did you?" he asked.

"I made a bargain." She clutched her medallion. "Needed the old woman's help."

Jem looked up at her. "Old woman?" Then he understood. She wasn't talking about the Castillo. She was talking about bringing him to St. Augustine. "You mean Aunt Winnie? But I thought you traded with her. For me."

"You got it turned around. Bringing you here was my payment to her."

"What?" This didn't make sense. "You're lying! What would you need to pay her for? You don't even believe in conjure."

BOOM! BOOM! BOOM! The Castillo walls shook. Someone said a prayer in rapid Spanish.

"I don't set store by her charms and potions. But others do. And I needed something. Not for me, for someone else."

"But how…?"

"Don't you see? All those folks coming to her for those beads and charms tell her things. Tell her what they need, what they know, what their problems are. That old busybody knows everything that happens in Charles Town and beyond. And she has power too. Those who believe in her charms will do anything she says."

"What did you want from her?"

"Influence enough to keep someone safe. But that old witch doesn't give nothing for free."

"She was good to me," Jem said. She *had* been good to him. Hadn't she?

"I'm not saying she wasn't. I know it was hard for her to lose you."

Jem puzzled over this. Then why had Aunt Winnie sent him away? "Was it because she wanted me to go to Mose where I'd be free?"

"Maybe so, but that's not what she told me. 'I'll keep your man from harm,' she said, 'but only if you take my boy Jemmy to St. Augustine before they kill him.'"

BOOM! BOOM! BOOM! The cannons sounded as though they were getting nearer. With every hit, the ground vibrated like a giant coming to life beneath them. The walls surrounding the courtyard rattled.

Jem heard the explosions, felt each impact, but it was as though they were happening somewhere far away. In his mind, he was back in Charles Town. Back at Master's house. In the kitchen with Aunt Winnie as she dabbed salve on his burns, set his broken bones, poured sassafras tea into a cup and watched as Jem drank it down. Was Phaedra telling the truth? Had Aunt Winnie made a bargain to save him from Master? Was that why he was here?

Kill him, kill him, kill him. The words were a battering chorus in Jem's ears. Was death the fate he'd escaped when he left Charles Town? And if so, what would happen if the Castillo fell to the English? If he survived the cannon fire, would he be taken back to Master's house? Jem looked around for a sign, but smoke and dust filled the yard. He searched the clear blue of afternoon far above, but there was nothing to suggest the Sky God was watching.

Lowering his gaze, he spied Juba peering down from the gun deck. *He's looking for Adine and Maria,* Jem thought, and waved to show where they were, huddled together just a few feet away. His eyes met Juba's for a moment and the older man's expression softened. Before disappearing back toward the harbor, Juba nodded and raised a fist into the air.

"*Ave Maria!*" someone called from across the yard. Jem turned to see who had spoken.

"*Ave Maria!*" another voice answered.

With each ball that hit, more voices joined in, until the chorus seemed almost strong enough to drown out the sound of the cannons.

When the guns and shouts stilled, he turned to Phaedra. "What about Aunt Winnie's part? Did she help you like she'd promised?"

"No!" Phaedra put her face in her hands and wept.

Chapter Twenty-Eight

June 14, 1740

The cannon fire stopped at dark, but the night did not promise much rest for those inside the Castillo. One of the Spanish gunners was hit, his leg shattered by an English cannonball. The poor man's cries filled the courtyard long after the deafening guns had gone silent.

Jem only fell asleep as the sky turned the deep blue of early morning and the stars began to fade.

When he awoke, Phaedra was no longer beside him. Lines had formed at the well and in front of the cook pot nearby. Jem wondered how long he had slept. He was powerful hungry, but before he looked for food, he wanted to inspect the yard and see how the Castillo fared after the long day of shelling.

Across the courtyard, he saw Big Sunday coming down the steps from the gun deck. Jem ran to meet him.

"You all right?" Big Sunday asked.

"Yessir," Jem said. "You?"

The captain nodded, but his face looked drawn, his eyes red.

Jem followed Big Sunday around the yard. Belongings were spread everywhere. Earlier attempts at order had been wiped out by the attack. But already groups of women were shaking and folding blankets, wiping and stacking bowls and spoons. Maribel and Phaedra were standing side by side, ladling scoops of water for the exhausted soldiers.

Jem noticed that the people of Mose no longer huddled together as a group. The invisible line that had separated them from the Spanish seemed to have disappeared in the night. Adine was rocking Maria in her arms and talking with a Spanish lady who held a boy about the same size.

The fear and sleeplessness of the previous night should have left folks short-tempered and out-of-sorts. But that wasn't what it looked like to Jem. Phaedra had even allowed Maribel to help her.

"What's everyone so happy about?" Jem asked.

"Not exactly happy," Big Sunday said. "More relieved. Many didn't think the Castillo would stand under English fire."

"What's it like outside?" Jem asked. "Is there lots of damage?"

"Some of the new stone shattered," Big Sunday said as they made their way along the wall toward a crowd gathered in the north corner. "But the man hit was the worst of it."

"Is he going to be all right?"

"Don't know," Big Sunday said. "He'll live, I think, and that's a blessing."

"*Ave Maria* must be a mighty powerful prayer," Jem said, "to have protected the Castillo from those cannonballs."

"Faith is a powerful thing," Big Sunday said. "I want to

show you something." He led Jem through the crowd to where a cannonball had come over the gun deck and crashed into a courtyard wall.

Jem gaped at the sight. Instead of shattering the stone, the cannonball had lodged there, burrowed into the wall like a spoon into a roasted yam. "Why didn't it break?"

"Look carefully," Big Sunday told him.

Jem ran his hand over the wall. There were small flecks in it he'd never noticed before. "It's not solid rock." He leaned in close. "Looks like pieces of seashell."

"It's called coquina," Big Sunday said. "It's made naturally by shifting sands over thousands of years. Domingo's people first showed the Spanish where to find it. There's a quarry across the bay where they dig and cut the coquina while it's still soft. Over time, it hardens."

"How can a bunch of tiny shells make a stone that eats cannonballs?" Jem asked.

"They may be little shells," Big Sunday said, "but stuck together, they're strong."

⸺ ⸺

Jem slept fitfully that night. The dreams returned. This time he was hiding from Master in the coal chute of the Charles Town house. He wasn't sure what it was he'd done, but he knew Master was going to whip him. His back still burned from the last time; the cuts hadn't had a chance to heal. It was dark and cold and he could hear footsteps coming closer. But then he heard her voice. "Jemmy, you in there?"

Jem woke up with a start. It was clear to him now. Aunt Winnie had wanted to save him just like he'd wanted to save Omen from the crows. She'd put herself at risk to pay for his freedom and he hadn't even thanked her. If only he could see her again.

Rousing himself, Jem went to get some water. As he often did, he checked his pockets to make sure the magnifier and the whistle were still there. They were. He pulled out the whistle and blew on it softly. Where was Omen now? he wondered, looking up at the early morning sky. Then another thought struck him. What if Omen flew into Mose? The English would shoot him, just like the Spanish shot the other owl. Jem's chest pounded. He couldn't let that happen. He had to find a way to search for Omen.

But how would he get out of the Castillo? Jem wandered around the yard and then hung around the entrance for a while, trying to think of what to do. As he watched Rojas talking to a group of Spanish soldiers, the answer became clear.

He would walk out the same way he'd entered: across the drawbridge.

Jem quietly made his way to the group and stood behind the general. "Pardon, sir," Jem said, tugging on the tail of his jacket.

"What is it?" The general looked annoyed.

"Um…Phaedra told me you'd never allow it, but I—"

"Allow what? That woman does not speak for me."

"Yessir," Jem said. "I told her that, sir, but she wouldn't listen to me. I want to help. I can scout the area for you. I know of a tree I can climb and see over the walls right into Fort Mose."

The general glared at him. "What makes you think you'd be a better scout than our militiamen?"

"I don't, sir. It's just that it's a mighty thin poplar that wouldn't hold the weight of a grown man. And remember, it was me that spotted them last time. Now, Phaedra said you wouldn't agree—"

"Do not speak that name again. Go! Climb your tree. I doubt you'll see anything of use to us, but it won't hurt to try." He pointed toward the gate. "Guards," he said, "let the boy pass."

It was that easy.

Once outside, Jem stood for a moment, gulping the briny air. He'd never noticed how wonderful it tasted. He spread his arms and ran, the feeling of space and movement making him lightheaded after so much time cramped in the yard of the Castillo.

He turned back and surveyed the walls. What had he been thinking all those months when he'd longed to get inside? Still, they had protected them from the English cannons, and for that Jem was grateful. There was movement inside a small opening in the bastion. He hoped it wasn't one of the men from Mose on guard duty. He needed to get away before someone saw him and told Phaedra.

Outside the walls, Jem glanced over at the forest. There was no sign of Omen and no trail of smoke from the woods where Shadrack kept his kiln. To the north, there was no movement from the direction of the Indian village, no one to kick up dust on the trail between town and Mose.

Jem was on his own.

He hadn't lied to the general. He would climb the tree and look over at Mose. But first he would search for Omen.

Instead of taking the trail toward Mose, Jem headed for the fields. He hoped his straw-colored shirt and brown pants would help him blend in as he made his way through the dried cornstalks.

He glanced over at the tree line, and had the unsettling feeling that he was being watched. He told himself it was silly, that if there were any eyes on him, it was probably just those of a squirrel or a tree frog. Still, he rubbed the beads on his shirt and stayed in the cornfields where he'd be able to see danger coming.

Jem entered the forest when he got near the tall poplar tree. He ran to it and started climbing. Only when he got far up in the thick branches did he allow himself a deep breath.

Scanning the nearby treetops, he saw no sign of Omen. He pulled out the owl whistle and he blew one call…then another. He waited several moments, but there was no answer. Disappointed, he looked in the direction of Mose.

Jem smiled at first to see the watchtower peeking over the walls, the round roofs of the chosas. He hadn't realized how much he'd missed the fort.

But when he looked more closely, the grin froze on his lips. The fort's walls had been taken down in several places. Men in red coats strolled through the yard, moving in and out of the chosas and around the well. Were they the same troops he'd seen marching in Charles Town? Jem's stomach went sour. His mouth tasted bitter. He spat. One of those soldiers was sleeping in his bed.

He had a lot to report to General Rojas. He pulled out the owl whistle again and blew. Once, twice, three times.

Jem peered out at the forest for any glimpse of movement in the trees. Nothing.

Then he heard voices in the distance.

When he looked back down toward Mose, he saw a group of soldiers approaching the gate from the north. The sound of their laughter rose through the leaves, tightening the knot in Jem's innards. As they came closer, he blinked hard, nearly losing his grip

There must be some mistake.

Jem leaned forward to get a better look. There was no mistake. Bobbing among the red jackets was the flash of a red cap.

A red possum cap.

The English had captured Reynard! But even as Jem grasped at the notion, he knew it was false. Knew it from the way Reynard patted one of the Englishmen on the back and tilted his head to laugh.

He wasn't their prisoner, he was their friend!

Jem felt as if a giant bellows had sucked the breath from his chest. Phaedra was right. He had been a fool.

Reynard was a spy.

The smell of roasted venison wafted up from Mose. And then with a rush that made his heart pound, Jem remembered the times he'd talked with the trader about food and cannons.

He'd given Reynard the information the English needed to destroy St. Augustine! There was no need to overpower the Castillo with more guns. All they had to do was sit back and wait until the food ran out.

The Castillo would fall, but not under English fire. It would fall to hunger. Now the English could just bide their time.

Jem scrambled down the trunk. He had to get back to the Castillo.

"Halt!"

The unmistakable click of a musket stopped him in his tracks.

Chapter Twenty-Nine

June 18, 1740

Jem was shoved toward the yard, a musket barrel jabbing into his back.

"It's all right," Reynard said. "I know the boy."

Jem glared at him.

"Let us talk alone for a moment, Brock," Reynard told the soldier. "I believe the boy may have news for me."

"He's my prisoner, trader. Don't forget it." Brock pushed Jem forward with his gun.

"We meet again," Reynard said. "Good to see you, my friend."

Jem didn't answer. He scanned the tree line for signs of Omen.

"I'm glad you've come." Reynard patted Jem on the shoulder. "Could see as soon as I met you that you were a man like me."

"Like you?" Jem repeated.

"We're survivors. Both of us."

"I am not like you," he said. "You're a spy."

Reynard laughed. "Don't be naïve. I'm a trader. I trade in goods and I trade in information. You and I have exchanged both. You've been very helpful."

"You tricked me!" Jem said. "I never would have told you anything if I'd known you were on their side."

"I'm not on their side," Reynard said. "I'm not on anyone's side."

"You betrayed me! I'm not like you. I'd never betray a friend."

"Is that what you think the Spanish are? Your friends? Do you truly believe they care about you?"

"Yes." But even as he spoke, Jem thought of what Phaedra had said. If she was right about Reynard, could she be right about the Spanish too?

"Then you're not as clever as I thought. They drew you here, all of you, to put some bodies between them and the English. That and to fan the flames of rebellion up north. And look at the vexation it's caused. All those people enslaved up in Charles Town, burning to get down here. They're the ones who caused this war. Or you could say it was the Spanish who caused it by offering up freedom. All I know is, I had nothing to do with it."

"You were the one hiding in the woods! You must have been waiting to meet one of the English scouts. You were the one who hit me!"

"I don't know what you're talking about," Reynard said. "I'd never strike a child."

"Liar!" Jem's head hurt.

"Don't you see?" Reynard asked. "Folks like you and me are alone in this world. We have to look out for ourselves."

"Even if it means betraying people?"

"I don't see it that way," he said. "I owe it to myself to make the best trade possible. At present, the English are the ones with the heaviest purses."

"You're not so clever," Jem said. "Others at Mose saw through you, even if I didn't."

"You mean Phaedra? She hates everyone, you included. Look." Reynard reached for Jem's ear.

"Don't touch me."

"I was only going to give you this." Reynard held out a gold coin.

"What for?"

"You earned it. I got it from Colonel Palmer, the commander of the English troops here, for the information you gave me about the food stores."

"I don't want it."

Reynard raised his eyebrows. "And here I'd had the notion we could become partners. Been looking for a lad I could teach the business to, someone I could take along with me on my travels."

Jem thought of the time, not long ago, when he would have given anything to hear those words. What a fool he'd been! "I'd never go anywhere with you!"

Reynard shook his head. "I'm very sorry we can't do business."

Jem gazed around at the once-familiar yard. The well, the watchtower, the notched beam where Omen had perched.

Now everything felt strange and forbidding. "I'll be leaving now."

Reynard laughed, the soft fur of his possum cap rippling in the breeze. "That could be a bit tricky. If the Spanish were to get wind that the English are waiting them out, they might decide to do something rash." He brought two fingers to his mouth and whistled. "Brock," he called. "Your prisoner isn't enjoying our company."

—————

The fire burned hot in the center of the yard. Jem hadn't been offered stew, but he wouldn't have eaten it anyway.

He'd been led to a chosa and handed over to a thin English soldier with a pinched face and a fancy uniform. "My name is Colonel Palmer," the man said. "I have some questions for you."

Jem kept his head down and stared at the floor.

"Where did you live before you came to St. Augustine?"

Jem put on his best houseboy face. "Don't recall," he muttered.

"Bring in the trader," Palmer called.

Soon Reynard joined them in the chosa. "The boy came from Charles Town."

"Who was your master?" the colonel asked Jem.

"Master?" Jem asked dumbly.

"The boy is afraid to talk," Reynard said. "The Spanish have probably threatened him."

"Is this true?" Palmer asked Jem.

Jem tried to look confused, first nodding, then shaking his head.

"We won't harm you if you cooperate," Palmer whispered in his ear. Jem shrunk from the foul smell of his breath.

"I doubt the boy knows anything more than he's already told me," Reynard said. "The people here didn't seem to trust him. They'd have watched what they said around this one."

Jem felt as though he'd been struck. What Reynard had said about him was true. He wasn't to be trusted.

"We'll give you some time to think about this." Palmer beckoned to a soldier, who took Jem by the collar. "You'll see that we English do not give up so easily."

Despite Jem's struggle, the soldier led him away and shut him in a small chosa.

Jem sat quietly on the floor of the empty hut for what seemed like hours. He was starving. There was no use trying to find a way out; this was one of the chosas that had been used for storing grain and it didn't even have an opening to let air in. Jem was on his hands and knees in the dark searching for a place where he might dig his way out when he heard someone approaching. He sat up and faced the door.

Without a word, Brock entered, jerked him to his feet, and led him outside. The night was dark. A group of men stood around the campfire.

"If you won't talk, you'll have to entertain the troops with a jig." Brock pushed him into the circle toward the fire. "Who has a flute?"

From the other side of the fire came a delicate melody. It struck Jem as out of place.

"This is your last chance to tell us something worthwhile," Brock said.

Again Jem put on his Charles Town mask. He made his eyes go vacant, his mouth slack.

"Why don't we start with how much food, how many cannons, and how much gunpowder the Spanish have?"

Jem stared into the fire, determined not to give in.

"Still can't remember? Then I suppose you'll just have to show us your best jig." Brock pulled a burning stick from the fire and held it close to Jem's feet. "Step lively," he said, laughing. "Go on!"

Jem tried to move his feet, but he felt as though he were walking in water up to his neck.

The soldiers jeered.

"You'll have to do better than that!" Brock called.

It was no use. Jem swayed a bit, but his legs had turned to stone.

"Dance!" the soldiers shouted again and again. The chorus of their voices rang in his ears.

Brock lunged at him with the stick, its tip glowing fiery red. Another soldier picked up a smoldering piece of firewood and jabbed Jem in the ribs. A searing pain tore through his gut. He lurched, the smell of the burnt cloth making his stomach roil.

The faces around the fire blurred. The sneering mouths

and clapping hands became a jagged line at the edge of Jem's vision, a wail in his ears. The old fear was all he could feel. He was back in Charles Town; he knew it from the smell of burnt flesh and by the laughter.

He fell forward. Reynard caught him. His face was so close that Jem could smell the stew on his breath. "Play along," Reynard whispered through clenched teeth.

The trader pulled Jem upright. "That won't do!" he said in a loud voice. "You must give these gentlemen a proper show!"

Jem felt a yank at his neck.

Reynard was holding his owl whistle up for the soldiers to see. "*Bon*. His whittling skill has improved!" he said. "I wonder just what the owl design signifies?" He raised his eyebrows.

Jem grabbed for it. Too slow.

"Shhhh!" Reynard waved his arms and the music stopped. He raised the whistle to his lips and blew.

Once, twice, three times.

When the whistling stopped, Jem could hear nothing but the blood beating in his ears.

Reynard looked disappointed. The men began to talk again.

Jem drew a ragged breath, willing his heart to calm down. Omen had not heeded the call. He'd not been lured from the safety of the forest.

In the trees outside the walls, a crow cried and another replied. A breeze blew in from the marsh.

That's when he heard the faraway sound.

Chapter Thirty

June 18, 1740

From the darkness beyond the walls of the fort came an answering call. Faint at first, low and hollow, but growing stronger.

Jem prayed it was his imagination.

Reynard grinned. "Gentlemen, the boy's dancing has been a disappointment. But all is not lost. Watch as I conjure an owl out of the night air." He made a sweeping gesture with his arms and thrust his hands toward the sky.

The soldiers gazed at the sky, spellbound.

Let it not be Omen, Jeb chanted to himself. *Let it not be Omen. Not Omen…not Omen…not Omen…*

A shadow passed over the yard. Someone cried out. Jem wasn't sure if it was his own voice he heard.

"Don't shoot, lads," Reynard said. "The creature is the boy's pet. It's tame."

Omen landed with a grace that shocked Jem. How beautiful and proud the owl looked. He'd become all Jem had hoped for him, and more. Regal and strong, his gaze met Jem's.

"A fine-looking bird," said Brock. "Who is the best shot around here?"

Dread filled Jem's throat. "No!" he screamed. The soldiers on either side grabbed his arms. "Fly away!" He squeezed his eyes shut, willing Omen not to be there when he opened them.

But Omen stayed.

Reynard untied the rawhide string that held the whistle. He dropped the whistle and advanced toward Omen, holding the length of string behind his back.

Omen turned his head and stared at Jem.

"Leave him be!" Jem cried. Brock cuffed him hard on the head and Jem fell to the ground.

When he sat up, he saw Reynard coming back to the fire, carrying Omen by his feet. The rawhide string dangled from one of Omen's talons like a leash.

"Since the boy can't dance, let's see if the bird will oblige." Reynard knelt to set the owl down.

The soldiers began to chant. "Dance, dance, dance!"

Someone threw a pebble. It bounced off Omen's head and he staggered.

"Stop!" Jem tried to reach Omen but someone seized his collar and pulled him back. He landed hard on the ground. The wound in his side pulsed with pain.

"Patience," said Reynard. "That's not the way to get an owl to dance." He pulled hard on the leather strap, yanking Omen toward him.

The confused owl lost his balance. He beat his wings and tried to right himself, shrieking in protest.

"This is how." Reynard grabbed a stick from the fire. Its tip smoked and glowed orange. He pushed it toward the owl. Just like the soldier had done to Jem.

Omen made a growling sound.

Reynard waved the burning stick slowly back and forth.

The owl snapped his beak and flapped his wings.

Reynard prodded again, the tip of the stick poking at the soft white feathers on Omen's legs.

Jem clenched his hands into fists, fingernails digging into his palms.

Omen had begun to sway side to side, big yellow eyes blinking.

"*Voilà!*" Reynard cried. "I've taught the bird to dance."

Laughter and cheers went up around the circle.

Jem kept his eyes locked on Omen. Glaring at Reynard, the owl raised his wings. His plumage ruffled and he appeared to grow larger. The feather horns on the top of his head stood straight on end.

The crowd roared their approval.

Reynard pulled on the string again. Omen lurched forward.

Jem held his breath.

Omen clacked his beak. He made a few short barking cries.

Jem moved quietly, getting to his knees, then to his feet. No one seemed to notice. All eyes were on the owl.

"Listen!" Reynard cried. "Seems I've taught him to sing as well!" He threw his head back and laughed.

The voices around the fire merged into a roar.

The owl rose into the air, wings spread to their full reach, and hovered for a moment. The soldiers stared up at him, their throats illuminated by the firelight.

A true predator senses its prey's weakness. Knows instinctively when to strike.

Omen descended on Reynard like an avenging angel. It happened so quickly, the soldiers were caught off guard.

But not Jem.

Omen drove his talons into Reynard's throat and slashed at his face with his beak.

Jem dove into the circle and grabbed the tether from Reynard's hand, the trader's screams sounding in his ears.

Jem landed hard, his forehead hitting the packed earth. "Fly, Omen!" he screamed, tossing the rawhide string in the air. He heard wings flapping and felt the soft touch of feathers brushing across his cheek.

When he looked up, Omen was already above him, a dark silhouette against the yellow and orange flames. Higher and higher he rose.

A part of Jem rose with him, and for a moment he was gazing down at Mose with owl's eyes. Powerful wings pulled at the air, bending, shaping it to his will.

Omen flew out across the yard and toward the forest, the rawhide tether still dangling from his foot.

And then he was gone.

On his hands and knees, Jem backed away from the circle. A stone bit into his palm. Not a stone—the whistle. He held it tight in his fist as he scrambled to his feet.

The soldiers leapt to try to help Reynard. Moaning in pain, the trader rocked back and forth, hands over his eyes.

Dark lines of blood spilled from between his fingers and ran down the back of his hands.

"You!" Brock turned toward Jem with his bayonet raised.

Jem stepped backward, tripped over the bench at the edge of the circle, and fell, right leg folding awkwardly beneath him. A dagger of pain sliced into his thigh.

"Get up!" Brock poked the bayonet into Jem's chest.

Jem started to rise, but sank again. "My leg!" he cried. "It's broke!"

"Lemme see." One of the soldiers leaned down and grabbed it.

"Noooo!" Jem screamed, surprised at how strong his voice sounded.

"I barely touched him," the soldier said, backing off. "Best get the doc to take a look."

"We don't need to waste doctoring on this one," another said. "Too puny to be worth much."

"Might have been worth something without the broke leg," a third answered.

"Why'd you have to break his leg?" the first soldier asked.

"Not me," said Brock. "Fool did it to himself."

"Whoever did it, did it. I'd a done worse," the second said. "Boy doesn't deserve to live after what his bird did."

"Palmer thinks he knows something."

Brock grunted. "Don't believe it. Besides, who would've told anything to a little runt like this?"

"What'll we do with him now? Can't march him back to Charles Town with a broke leg."

"Kill him, I suppose."

Jem tested his toes, wiggling them in his boots.

"It's not for you to decide," Brock pointed out.

"Colonel Palmer said not to harm him."

"That old windbag? Makay's the one in charge. He'll be back soon."

"We'll say it was an accident. Let's just finish him off now and have done with it."

"I'll not risk it."

"Nor me."

"Well, then. What do we do with him in the meantime?"

The blade of the bayonet prodded his leg. Jem winced but otherwise kept still.

"He ain't going anywhere, is he?"

"Suppose not."

"We can decide in the morning. Let's get some sleep."

It was only when all the soldiers had disappeared that Jem allowed himself a full breath. Gradually, the sounds around him died away. The fire burned down to glowing embers.

Something fluttered to the ground beside him. A feather. He marveled that it had survived, still white and pristine.

His side ached and the pain in his leg was a dull throb. But like Omen, Jem must be patient. He lay there, thinking about what he must do next.

After what seemed like hours, Jem heard voices.

"I'm telling you, we need to rouse them."

"Let them sleep. We've had a drill every night. And for what?"

"To be ready to do battle, that's what."

"Not in the middle of the night, they don't. Not on half rations."

"Are you refusing?"

"I am."

Jem heard the two men's boots on the packed mud.

He closed his eyes. Anyone walking past would believe him asleep. Or dead.

The yard went quiet again.

Still, he bided his time, waiting as the silence stretched.

Though he was afraid, the numbness was gone.

When the yard had been still for what seemed like an hour, Jem got to his feet. He carefully took a step...then another.

Omen's broken wing trick had worked!

Chapter Thirty-One

June 19, 1740

I t's all my fault," Jem said. It was first light the next day, and Jem and Big Sunday were in the governor's room at the Castillo.

The governor glared at him. "The trader?" he asked. "The one with the possum hat?"

Jem nodded. "I told him there were about twenty cannons and only enough food for a month."

"I must take the blame," Big Sunday said. "I was the one the boy heard it from."

The governor's face was drawn, his cheeks hollow. "I'm disappointed in you, Captain. I expected better."

Big Sunday bowed his head. "Boy says there are about a hundred troops, well-armed and supplied."

"Well, that's something, at least. And now we know that since they couldn't break us with their guns, the English are planning to wait us out." The governor wiped a hand across his face. "They won't need to wait long."

As they left the governor's quarters, Jem caught up with Big Sunday. "I'm sorry," he said. "How can I make it right?"

Big Sunday's voice was flat. "You've done all you could, and I'm sure you weren't the only one taken in by the trader."

"I'm not ready to face the others yet," Jem said.

Big Sunday nodded. "You can go help with the animals in the moat."

Grateful, Jem headed toward the gate.

He was assigned to cleaning up dung. Jem's weary eyes watered as he pushed a rake among the few cows and sheep that remained. It was a mercy that most had already been slaughtered. The moat was now a dusty pit with nothing green for them to graze on.

By midmorning, the day turned hot. Flies swarmed around his face. He finished raking and leaned against a shady spot of the Castillo wall.

He wondered where Omen was at that moment. Jem raised the whistle to his lips and blew. *"Whooo, whooo—"* He dropped the whistle.

If Omen came to the Castillo, he'd be shot!

He held his breath and waited. Luckily, there was no answering call.

Reynard was right; the English would win by starving them out.

"Move along!" one of the militiamen shouted at Jem. "If you've no more work to do, get out of our way." Jem headed back to the courtyard. He couldn't put off facing the others any longer.

He saw Phaedra first, sitting in the shade against the

courtyard wall, working on a small basket. Jem wondered if her supply of grass was almost gone as well.

Maribel sat beside her, with what appeared to be the beginnings of her own basket.

"Stop your gawking." Phaedra leaned over to inspect Maribel's work. "You have to make the rows tight. Else they won't hold together."

Jem stared at them, chest pounding like a drum. Phaedra's words repeated in his head: *make the rows tight else they won't hold*. He thought of being up in the tree, gazing down at Fort Mose. Why hadn't it occurred to him before? He ran to find Big Sunday.

Jem, Big Sunday, the governor, Rojas, and the leader of the Spanish militia stood around a table strewn with maps.

"I forgot to tell you," Jem said. "They've torn down sections of the wall around the fort."

"Why would they have done that?" the governor asked.

"To keep it from being used as a defense," Big Sunday said. "Likely did it before they decided to camp there themselves. Before they found out how little food we have."

Jem shifted uncomfortably.

"Can you draw us a map of where the walls are breached?" Big Sunday asked.

"Yes, sir."

The governor pushed a piece of parchment forward. Big Sunday handed him a quill.

Jem tried to picture Mose as it had appeared to him, look-ing down from the tree. He drew a square. "This is the north wall," he said, pointing to the top line. "This part's been taken down." He made a mark on the square. "It's also breached here, and here along the east wall."

"Is the lad to be believed?" Rojas asked. He paced back and forth in the governor's room in the Castillo, casting tall shadows against the far wall in the light of the lone lantern. "Or is he perhaps trying to impress us with more tales of his cleverness?"

"I'm telling the truth," Jem protested. "I just didn't remem-ber about the walls until—"

"If he's correct," the Spanish commander said, "the Mose militia and the Spanish troops have a chance to retake the fort."

"Agreed," Big Sunday said. "But not without the Indians."

"Are there any still about?" Rojas said. "I heard they'd all run away."

Big Sunday turned to the governor. "You know that's not true. They know these parts better than we do, and they've fought Palmer before. We must do this together. It won't work any other way."

"I just thought of something else," Jem said. "I heard two English officers arguing. One wanted the troops to rise in the night, the other said they were worn out and should be allowed to sleep." He remembered how Omen did his best hunting just before dawn. "They'll be most vulnerable before daylight."

"It doesn't matter," the governor said. "Even with the information the boy has given us, even with the help of the

Indians, we still cannot mount an attack."

"Why not?" Rojas said.

"We don't have enough arms."

"We don't need more muskets," Big Sunday said. "Swords will do."

The governor sighed. "Our charcoal has run out. We've no way to forge more weapons. Without them, there's no hope of taking the fort back."

There was a knock on the door. "What is it?" the governor called.

"A maroon from Mose," the guard said. "Just got here and wants to see the captain."

Big Sunday moved toward the door. "Might as well send him in."

As the door opened wider, Jem's nose twitched. He didn't need to look up to know who had arrived

"We'd given you up for dead," Big Sunday said.

Shadrack squinted in the dim light. "You'd look dead, too, if you'd been out there working all by yourself. Didn't have time to sleep, let alone be dead." He was a sight, his hands and face covered in soot and his clothes blackened as well.

"You were tending your kiln while the English marched in?" the governor asked.

Shadrack went on as though he hadn't heard the question. "I was tending the kiln when they came. Finished a whole cartload the day those scoundrels marched in."

"It's a pity we don't have it now," the governor said.

"You think I left it behind?"

"What are you saying?" Big Sunday asked.

"I'm saying I brought it with me. Whole cart full."

Rojas sniffed. "Impossible. How did you make it through?"

Shadrack chuckled. "I heard an owl hoot over my right shoulder. Sounded like it was coming from the Castillo. When I looked, there wasn't much smoke rising, so I suspicioned your charcoal was almost gone. Good luck that owl come along when it did. I seen the English come in one side of the woods, so I took my load of charcoal to the other side. Been biding my time there since, hiding out and waiting for a chance to haul it thisaways."

"Gentlemen," Big Sunday said. "We have an attack to plan."

"Get that charcoal to the forge," the governor told the guard at the door.

"Help Shadrack," Big Sunday said to Jem.

As Jem led Shadrack out the door, he heard the governor whisper to Big Sunday, "What was that dreadful smell?"

When they got out to the yard, Jem turned to Shadrack. "You found your conjure bag?" he asked.

The old man patted his chest. "How else could I have made it around those red-coated devils?"

—◦—

"Can't you see? I *have* to go," Jem said. "It was me that started it."

Big Sunday's expression softened. "You didn't start this. Plenty of causes, but you aren't one of them."

212

"But I told them—"

Big Sunday shook his head, his "no" barely audible over the din of hammering. Using the charcoal from Shadrack, the blacksmiths had worked through the night to forge blades.

Jem hung his head. "Please let me try to make up for the problems I've caused."

"You have done enough. We have your map."

"Why not let me fight?"

"I can't send you to fight," Big Sunday said. "You've never loaded a musket, much less fired one. It would be murder."

"Wait." Jem had just noticed Domingo standing nearby with a small bundle of kindling.

"I told you, I can't allow it," Big Sunday said.

Jem looked closer and Domingo was not carrying kindling. He was actually holding atlatls. The ones Jem had carved.

"We need another spear thrower," Domingo said.

Chapter Thirty-Two

June 26, 1740

A sliver of moon hung like a gleaming dagger over St. Augustine's harbor. There was no other light. The governor had ordered no fires be lit, lest the English take notice. Women lined the walls of the Castillo courtyard to say goodbye. None but the youngest children would sleep this night.

Phaedra leaned in close to Jem and whispered, "It's not too late—"

"I won't change my mind," he said.

"It's a man's decision," she said. "I reckon you're ready to make it."

Jem took a deep breath. This was what he'd longed for, what he'd planned for all these months. And while he would always remember Phaedra's words, the feeling they gave him wasn't what he'd expected. Instead of lighter and freer, he felt heavy and solid. He was still scared, but he also knew that, if it came to it, he'd shed his last drop of blood. Not for a faraway king, but for his people and their freedom.

His chest fluttered like a swarm of mayflies. But his hands were steady. "I am ready," he said, and meant it. He'd do what needed done.

"Papa, be careful," Maribel said. "*Cuidado.*"

Jem didn't hear him reply. The general was already walking toward the sally port.

"You certain of the hour?" Big Sunday asked Jem for the third time.

From Aunt Winnie's teaching, Jem could judge the time of night by the position of the stars. "I'm certain."

He crossed the drawbridge, the sound of footfalls on the wood echoing into the moat. A cow lowed and shuffled below. A sign of what was to come? Jem shook his head; he was done relying on conjure to determine his future.

Once on the other side of the Castillo walls, the forces split into three groups—the Mose militia, the Spanish troops, and the men from Domingo's village. Each would approach Mose from a different direction.

Spears and atlatl at his side, Jem followed Domingo and his men into the darkness. They approached Mose from the southwest, fanning out among the dry cornstalks as they neared. Then they waited.

The smell of pine smoke hung in the air: the only sound was the steady chirp of the cicada. Mose was quiet.

An animal scurried through the rows of stalks. A possum, or maybe a raccoon. Jem imagined he was an owl, high on a tree branch, invisible against the foliage. Watching, waiting.

In the predawn light, the walls looked higher than he

remembered, but he was relieved to see that his memory had been accurate. The Spanish soldiers and militia had his sketch; they knew exactly where the breaches were.

To his left, Domingo and two others knelt. The burning coals they'd carried from the Castillo jumped to life as each lit the torch attached to the end of his spear. A row of steady flames glowed in the darkness.

When it was his turn, Jem stepped forward and lit the torch. His breath came shallow and his fingers trembled slightly.

They fanned out, flames rising higher as they moved across the dark fields.

Jem's pulse pounded in his ears. His mouth had gone dry. The light from the flame made him feel exposed and vulnerable. But there was power in the fire as well. He set the flaming spear in the atlatl and breathed deeply. Flames licked at his left hand and wrist. He held fast.

A near-perfect imitation of a whippoorwill's call cut through the night.

The signal.

Summoning every bit of strength he had, Jem took a deep breath, then lunged. The flaming spear flew into the darkness, joining other fiery trails arcing high through the cornfield, across the ditch, and over the walls of Fort Mose.

For a moment, all was still. Then a shout rang out from inside the fort.

Jem picked up another spear.

He heard someone behind him mumble a prayer in Spanish, then the battle cry rang out and soldiers surged past.

"Fire! Fire!" The call came from inside the fort. Already,

an orange glow could be seen over Mose, as if the sun were rising. The fort was burning.

Silhouetted against the flames, the militia and soldiers charged though the gaps in the walls.

Musket balls ripped through the air. Jem heard shouts, screams, and curses in English and Spanish.

He pictured Big Sunday and the rest of the militia inside, fighting for their lives. For their freedom.

Jem ran toward the wall. There was no need to get to the nearest breach; instead, he used his old handholds and reached the top in seconds. There, he paused. He'd promised to go back to the woods after the torches were launched.

But what if the militia needed help? He might not be able to fire a musket, but he still had the atlatl and his knife. He'd already let them down. How could he take the chance of doing it again?

The yard below was a mass of bodies, surrounded by walls of flame and thick smoke. Swords clashed and muskets fired. Men knelt to reload; others fought hand-to-hand, wielding musket stocks as bludgeons, stabbing at each other with bayonets, or grappling on the ground. Some wore uniforms, others didn't. How could they tell friend from foe?

Jem looked for the red cap, but Reynard was nowhere to be seen.

Light glinted off a Spanish helmet—Rojas was squared off against a much larger English soldier, swinging his bayonet wildly. The Englishman had the advantage. He bore down on the general, pushing him toward a flaming chosa.

"Watch out!" Jem shouted.

The general stumbled over a fallen soldier, musket tumbling from his grasp. He landed on his back. The English soldier advanced.

Jem raised his spear. He tried to stand on the top of the wall, but the logs shifted beneath his feet. By the time Jem had regained his balance, the Englishman had drawn his sword from its scabbard and was rushing at Rojas. It was too late for Jem to aim again. The general was finished. But at that instant the English soldier stopped and pitched forward.

A third man came into view, stepping over the soldier's body and extending a hand to the general. In the light of the fire, the scar on his cheek seemed to glow.

Another shot rang out. Jem watched in horror as Juba dropped to his knees.

He scrambled over the wall and ran toward the wounded man. A dark spot was already spreading across his chest. He sank to the ground, still clutching his musket.

Jem put his arms under Juba's shoulders, trying to lift him. Juba shook his head.

"Let me help you," Jem pleaded.

Juba smiled. "To free," he said. Then his brow creased. "Shoulda...told someone," he muttered. "But I...I made a blood vow."

It was difficult to hear over the sounds of the battle. Jem leaned in closer. "Told what? What vow?"

"In the woods." Juba's voice was fading.

"What is it? Did you see the shadow that attacked me?"

"Thought you might've seen—"

There was a crash as a burning chosa fell to the ground.

Jem leaned over Juba to protect him from the flying embers. "Seen what?" Jem whispered. "Tell me what's out there!"

But Juba was gone.

Jem set Juba down gently, folding his arms over his chest. He stood just in time to see an English soldier bearing down on him.

Brock!

Jem grabbed Juba's musket and swung. The stock struck Brock full in the mouth. He staggered, dazed, small red eyes squinting.

A stream of blood flowed from the corner of the man's mouth. He spit and stared stupidly at the ground. "You've broken my tooth!" he cried.

"Stand back or I'll shoot!" Jem said.

Brock took a step closer. "I don't think so. Little runt like you? Bet you don't even know how." He prodded Jem's ankle with the tip of his bayonet. "Leg wasn't broken after all, eh?"

Jem felt the sting on his skin, the trickle of warm blood.

"I'll not trouble Colonel Palmer," Brock said, raising his bayonet. "For he's dead."

As Jem gaped at it, a shadow passed overhead. At first he thought it was his imagination, or a vision before death. But Brock must have seen it, too. He lifted his gaze.

A calm washed over Jem. He raised Juba's musket, and lashed out at Brock with the bayonet, slashing him across the thigh.

Brock bellowed and swung his musket.

Jem dropped to the ground and rolled away as the blade struck the dirt beside him. He scrambled to his feet and pressed the bayonet tip to Brock's chest. He didn't feel powerful, not the way he'd imagined he would. Real fighting wasn't like that. Instead, he felt a surge of energy, a desperate pounding, and a sickening fear.

Brock's face glowed white in the firelight. Small beads of sweat gathered on his forehead.

There was a splintering crash as another nearby chosa collapsed, releasing a shower of burning palm fronds. Jem jumped out of the way.

Brock batted at the embers with his free hand and ran toward the broken wall, dragging his injured leg.

Jem didn't try to stop him. All about the yard, bits of burning thatch rained down, glowing like fireflies.

Vengeful flames climbed the beams of the watchtower. Soon, its roof caught and the yard was illuminated as though by a giant torch. The heat and smoke made images waver and fade, fragile as a dream.

The fallen lay amongst the fire and ashes, some moaning and writhing on the dirt, others still.

Glancing over to where Juba lay, Jem felt a cannon's weight on his chest. Then he heard a familiar voice. Loud and measured, its deep timbre rose above the din of the battle.

Big Sunday and the militia had gained the advantage. English soldiers fled through the broken walls into the forest.

The battle was over. Jem gazed down at his hands. They shook slightly, and he noticed when he leaned against a solid section of the wall that his knees shook too.

He gazed around the ruined fort. Mose was empty of English, but still she burned.

Chapter Thirty-Three

June 29, 1740

They reached the Castillo as the first glimmer of the rising sun peeked over Anastasia Island. Jem had hoped they'd follow the eastern trail along the marsh so he could raise his spear in defiance at the English ships. But they didn't and he decided it was just as well; he was too tired to lift his arm.

The energy he'd felt after the battle had given way to numbness. Once he'd felt excited about driving the English from Mose, but now all he could think about was that Juba was gone and English ships still bobbed in the harbor.

Before the Castillo bridge was lowered to let them in, Jem asked Domingo to give him a boost so he could look over the eastern sea wall.

There, against the light of the rising sun, were the enemy ships. Seven of them, masts rising from the still waters like a palisade wall, separating St. Augustine from the channel to the ocean.

Jem took a deep breath of sea air and listened. Did the men out there know they'd lost Mose? *You couldn't take our home!* he wanted to shout to them. *We beat you!* But his voice wouldn't have carried. His throat was parched and his chest ached from the smoke. Domingo lowered him and they made their way to the passage through the thick walls of the Castillo. Two men from the Mose militia carried Juba's body to the dry moat to be prepared for burial along with the Spanish soldiers who'd died in the battle.

The yard was a tangle of shouts and movement as family members searched for each other.

Jem heard a strangled cry and looked over to see Big Sunday catch Adine as she sank to the ground. Phaedra was there, too, patting Adine's back with her long bony fingers, gentle in a way Jem had never seen them. His throat ached.

A trumpet sounded and the governor appeared on the gun deck above. It was hard to believe this was the same man who had spoken at the oath ceremony October last. Though Jem had seen him often since the siege began, he hadn't noticed until now how gaunt the governor's face had become, how his jacket hung as though made for a man twice his size.

"We welcome our brave heroes returned from battle. But we must continue to fight." The governor raised a fist. "The war is not yet won. We must break the hold of the English."

The heavy smell of smoke hung over the courtyard like a cloud. Jem gazed at the faces around him. The men who'd fought at Mose were red-eyed and covered in soot and ash. Some had burn marks on their clothing and wounded limbs wrapped in rags.

"Our food stores are almost gone," the governor continued. "I've sent word to Havana again, but until more supplies
arrive, we must conserve what little we have left for the soldiers who hold this fortress."

Jem stared at the women and children who'd run to meet
the militia. They were the ones the governor had ordered to
give up their rations so the soldiers might have strength
enough to fight. Their sunken eyes and hollowed faces told
of another kind of battle. A ribcage showing beneath a too-
big shirt. A red welt from an insect bite that wouldn't heal.
A cloth held up to bleeding gums.

How long would it be before others joined Juba? Dying
not a warrior's death as Juba had, but the slow kind, the
falling away of flesh until only bones remained?

Jem followed Big Sunday to the governor's quarters later
that day.

"We will not bury our dead in the moat," Big Sunday
insisted. "We will carry Juba to our burial ground and lay
him to rest there."

"That is too dangerous," the governor said. "The English
are still out there. If you're not shot, you could be held for
ransom or tortured in view of the Castillo."

"You owe us this. We'll go after dark, with my son and
other Indian warriors to scout for us."

Rojas clicked his tongue in disapproval, but the governor
consented. "We cannot help you if you are captured," he
warned. "I won't let the English use you to force our surrender."

"I would never ask you to do that," Big Sunday said.

It was just past midnight when they left the Castillo and

made their way west along the outer wall of St. Augustine.

In keeping with the old ways, they carried Juba's body to the burying ground by torchlight. The new moon cast a shimmery light over the path. To the south, St. Augustine lay empty and quiet, shuttered and sleeping behind the tall palisade.

Adine insisted on leaving the Castillo with them. "I will sing the funeral song and see my man buried properly," she said. She walked ahead of the robed priest who waved the incense decanter across the path. Domingo and the men from his village fanned out into the darkness.

The drumbeat started slow and quiet, then grew faster and louder. A wail pierced the night. Jem flinched, but the men carrying Juba's body never faltered.

Adine's voice rose as the mournful dirge began. *"Come quickly, let us work hard; the grave is not finished."*

Another voice, raw but strong, joined in.

"Sudden death cuts down the trees, let death be satisfied."

It was Phaedra. Jem had been surprised when she'd announced she'd be singing at the *teijami,* the ceremony for Juba crossing the river. Jem had been to plenty of buryings with Aunt Winnie, but Phaedra didn't keep with the old ways. He wondered how she even knew the song.

The singing continued and more voices joined in as they made their way down the path. The smell of smoke competed with the heaviness of the incense. Jem looked in the direction of Mose.

"Someone burning saw palmetto," Shadrack said. Walking beside Jem, he pointed east. "I'd know the smell anywhere. Wind's blowing it over from English camps on the island.

Fools probably think it'll keep mosquitoes away."

"Won't it?" Jem asked.

"Not as good as wax myrtle."

The incense made Jem feel light-headed. Now behind the woods and away from town, he could hear the rush of the river as it surged through the channel on its way to the ocean beyond.

The drums stilled and the singing stopped as they passed under a canopy of ancient oak. Hanging moss dangled from the limbs, forming a curtain that made him think of the night in the forest. That dark night when he'd first met Juba.

It seemed to Jem he was being carried on an irresistible course, like a fallen branch in the river. Swirling whirlpools might come to the surface here and there, but the force of the current always won in the end, relentlessly pushing toward the sea.

Aunt Winnie would know how to make sure Juba's spirit rested. But she wasn't here now. It was up to Jem. He checked his pocket. The things he needed were still there.

Dry leaves cracked under their feet as the procession entered the burying ground, following a trail between the plank and stone markers. Jem crossed himself as the priest had taught him.

The men carrying the casket set it down. Three others began to dig a grave.

In the glare of the lantern, Adine looked haggard, almost ghostly. When she'd sung, her voice had been so raw it had hurt Jem to listen. Now she swayed side to side, holding her empty arms as if cradling her baby, who was back at the Castillo. Her lips looked pale in the torchlight, moving as though she were speaking, but Jem heard no sound.

He tried to think of something to tell her, some comfort to offer. All that came to him were Juba's final words. *Blood vow. In the woods. Waiting.* What had he been trying to say?

Jem walked over to Adine and took one of her hands. It felt surprisingly warm. Her eyes, though sunken, were bright. "I was with him at the end, you know," Jem told her. He shifted, not sure how to continue. "He talked about that first night. When we met in the woods."

When she spoke, her voice filled the clearing. "None of you know what it cost Juba not being able to join the others at Stono. I can see him now, looking over his shoulder. He bore it on his back all those miles to free, and the weight of it bent him."

"He was a brave man," Big Sunday said.

"Yes," Adine said. "He paid a price to run instead of joining the rebellion. Only did it because he knew we'd never escape without him. For every one of you here, there's a thousand up there who can't never make it. Women with babies, old ones and young ones and hurt ones who can't run the miles and cross the swamps to free."

There was a long silence.

"I know some of you doubted us." She turned to face Phaedra. "Some of you still believe me and my man betrayed the rebellion to pay our way here."

Phaedra winced.

"I don't blame you for thinking it. Folks got to do what

they can for the ones who depend on them. And that's what Juba did for me and Maria. But he didn't betray anyone. And he spent his last breath fighting for freedom. I pray his soul rests peaceful."

"Amen," Phaedra said and others joined in.

The grave faced east, so Juba's spirit could find its way back to Africa.

Phaedra opened the covered basket she'd carried from the Castillo and took out a mortar and pestle. It was tradition to pound rice into flour as an offering to the dead. But there wasn't a grain of rice to be had in all of St. Augustine.

Jem watched as she bent and brushed the leaves from a spot on the ground. One by one, she collected acorns. When she had a handful, she dropped them into the mortar. To the sound of shovels heaving earth, Phaedra ground them into dust.

Big Sunday stepped forward. "Lord," he said. "We send our brother Juba home to you. While he walked your earth, he fought for right and for freedom."

The priest waved the incense holder in the sign of the cross, once, twice, three times. The fog of scented smoke made Jem dizzy. It was as though the secret Juba had guarded was hidden just outside the mist. The priest read last rites in Latin, his chants echoing through the clearing.

Then they were silent.

Juba was set to rest with his arms folded over his chest, a white shroud covering him. They formed a line and circled him, each resting a hand on his chest to say goodbye. Big Sunday and three other men lowered the body into the grave, then covered it with dirt. Finally the priest came forward and sprinkled on the holy water.

Adine set an upturned pot on top of the grave. An African sign of farewell.

The priest turned to lead the procession back to the Castillo.

Shadrack stepped up to the grave. He took broken pottery shards from his pockets and scattered them over the mound—offerings to release the spirit and prevent the soul from returning to the burial place. "From them who walk above the ground," he said, "to those who sleep beneath."

The drumming started again and Adine and Phaedra began a different song, less mournful than the first.

Jem crouched beside the grave, uneasy in the darkness. From his pocket, he took his own offering. Three of Omen's early feathers.

One by one, he stuck them upright into the earth covering Juba's casket.

As he turned to leave, there came a stirring from the river. The flapping of wings? No. It was more the sound of oars dipping into water. As though a spirit barge was coming to carry Juba's soul back across the sea.

And even though Jem had never seen Africa, and had never done anything truly brave or heroic, he sensed he was part of something bigger. It didn't matter that he was small or this-country-born. He was one of them now: a people who blended the stories of the past, the circumstances of the present, and the promise of the future into a whole greater than the sum of its parts.

"Jem?" Big Sunday's voice brought him back.

"Here," he called, and started toward the path.

A shout rang out as they re-entered the Castillo. By the time they'd gotten to the sally port, the cries were a chorus.

"What's going on?" Big Sunday asked one of the militia on guard duty.

"We're saved!" the man cried.

"How?"

"Shallow-draft boats. Governor sent them into the channel and out Matanzas inlet. Right under the English noses!"

Phaedra snorted. "Man's more clever than he looks."

The yard broke out into a cheer.

"Good people!" the governor called from the gun deck. He waited until the crowd stilled. "We have God and the tide on our side."

There were more shouts. The governor held up his hands.

"The English may have our harbor blocked, but their warships are no match for the speed and cunning of St. Augustine's sailors. Yesterday, I received word that our long-prayed-for supplies had arrived at a harbor down the coast. Early this morning, I sent twelve sailors into the shallows to fetch them. These brave men in their tiny boats fought past the English at Matanzas and returned with all the food we'll need to survive the siege."

The crowd cheered. Around him women wept. "*Ave Maria!*" they cried.

A tingling sensation spread up Jem's arms. He thought of Juba and what he had sacrificed to see his wife and child live free. Jem pictured Juba as he was in life, sitting tall and proud as his spirit barge glided across the Matanzas River. He imagined Juba holding up his hand to halt the English, and nodding to each of the supply boats as they passed on their way back to St. Augustine. He would have made sure it was so before his spirit left these shores and returned to its ancient home.

Chapter Thirty-Four

July 7, 1740

J em woke to Shadrack shaking him by the shoulders. "Big Sunday's calling for you."

He rubbed his eyes. A cry went up along the gun deck. It echoed through the bastions and down among the crowded courtyard. He jumped to his feet and headed toward the ramp.

Big Sunday stood near the top. He beckoned to Jem. "Come up here."

"Am I allowed?" Not waiting for a response, Jem took the stone stairs two at a time.

"You helped take back Mose," Big Sunday said. "You deserve to see this."

But see what? The sun hadn't yet risen, and the sky was still the deep purple of ripe mulberries. Damp and liquid, as though with just a stroke of a brush it could wash over the horizon and make the land disappear. Big Sunday pointed toward the bay and the channel beyond.

Jem drew in a sharp breath. He stared as the sails on the English ships grew smaller and smaller.

After thirty-eight days, the siege had ended.

In celebration, the governor ordered an allotment of rum for each soldier. General Rojas swaggered around the courtyard issuing orders.

"Ain't the rum," Phaedra said, as though she could read his mind. "Man's drunk on power. You would've thought he rowed those supply boats all by himself."

After the celebrating, there were decisions to be made. Where would the people of Mose live now that the fort had been destroyed? Would it be rebuilt?

Big Sunday was insistent. "We kept our vow. The militia of Mose defended St. Augustine. Juba paid with his life," he said. "Fort Mose must be rebuilt and the king owes us pay same as the other soldiers. If I have to sail to Spain to remind His Majesty, I will."

In the meantime, everyone from Mose would have to live in St. Augustine.

As soon as they were allowed to leave the Castillo, Jem headed back to the fort. In the light of day, the destruction was even more complete than he remembered. In places, the earthworks were still standing. In others, the timbers beneath the walls had caught fire and burned, leaving the caked mud that had protected them to collapse in dusty piles.

Amidst the ashes, a flash of red caught his eye.

A piece of Reynard's possum cap, trampled and muddy but unmistakable. Brushing off the ash and dirt, he wondered where Reynard was now. Jem tried to summon the rage he'd felt when they'd last met, but there was a hollow place where anger had once sparked, as if part of his insides had been consumed by flame and burned away.

He walked over to the place where Juba had fallen. Nothing but a smoothed patch of earth marked the spot. He stared at it until he realized he was looking for one of Aunt Winnie's signs. Still trying to understand why Juba had to die. Was there something Jem could have done to prevent it?

He looked up at the sky. A flock of pelicans flew east toward the sea.

What had Juba been trying to tell him when he died? He'd never know. All he could hope was that Juba's spirit was at rest with the ancestors.

It wasn't enough. Jem kicked a burnt piece of wood. It shattered into pieces, a gleam of white amid the black.

Brock's broken tooth.

He picked it up, brushed it off, and kept walking.

Farther along, he came upon the chicken coop, or what had once been the chicken coop. The roost was charred on three sides and the nesting beds scattered around it were black with soot. Jem bent to search for his collection, using a fragment of the fence that had surrounded the coop to scrape away some of the burned hay. Most of it turned to ash at his touch.

One nest pile was larger than the others. He took a deep breath and blew at it.

The ash cleared to reveal a section of basket, a small skeleton, and the snake's rattle. Blackened, but still intact. He took out his magnifying glass and examined each of the items he'd collected. Where was the sense in all of it? What did it mean?

He clawed at the packed dirt with the fence rail.

When he'd made a hole the size of his fist, Jem gently laid the bones, the rattle, the scrap of possum fur, and the tooth inside. He covered them with earth and ash, smoothing the surface with the palm of his hand. The remains of the charms would mix with the ashes of the old fort and make the new Fort Mose come up even stronger.

He got up and brushed his hands on his breeches. He must learn to let the past rest. Still, he couldn't help searching amid the ruins around the perimeter of the fort for whitewash and pellets. There was no sign Omen had been back.

But there were other signs of life at Mose.

Phaedra sat on a stump near the burned-out supports of their chosa, sewing a basket. The yard around her had been swept and cleared of weeds.

She didn't seem surprised to see him. "Our well made it through. Water's still salty." She handed him a cup. "But it tastes better to me than the water in St. Augustine."

"Thank you." Jem took a sip and gave the cup back. Phaedra was right. Their own water did taste better. "Surprised to see you without Maribel at your side."

"Hmmph. Child's got all she can handle looking after her fool of a father now that he's back at the Castillo with no one to boss." Phaedra shook her head. "She'll get him in line, though."

Jem was sure she would. He took the whistle from his pocket and faced the forest.

Whooo, whooo, whooo. The call echoed through the skeleton of the fort.

"You still haven't given up on that owl?" Phaedra asked.

"Can't seem to," Jem answered. "Can't shake the notion that he'll come back one day—even if just for a visit."

"Some things are hard to give up. Feels like letting go of a part of yourself, don't it?"

This made Jem pause. "I thought you hated it here. You said we were chickens set out here to squawk when the English came."

"And who was right about that?" She pointed the horn nail at him.

Jem smiled at the sign of the old Phaedra. "Why do you come back," he asked, "now that there's nothing here but ashes?"

"Got used to it, I reckon. Can't stand being stuck over there in St. Augustine. Can't breathe right."

"Aren't you afraid?"

Phaedra snorted. "What's there to be afraid of now?"

"Whatever was out there—"

"Probably nothing but wind and imagination," Phaedra said, but the hand holding her horn nail quivered. How strange that even the horn nail seemed less menacing now. Just a broken old spoon handle.

"A couple of times, I could've sworn Omen saw something," Jem said.

"If you can get him to come back and tell, then you're a better conjurer than that old woman in Charles Town."

At the mention of Aunt Winnie, they grew quiet.

"I thought Omen couldn't survive without me," Jem said, breaking the silence.

"You taught him well. Should be proud."

Jem nodded. "What you got in the bundle?" he asked, more to change the subject than because he was interested.

Phaedra looked up from her sewing. Was it his imagination, or had her weaving slowed? Though still sure, her fingers seemed to travel more carefully over the sweetgrass. "Just some things I wanted to have with me. See if I could set up out here."

"Think it'll be rebuilt?" Jem asked, looking around at the ruined fort.

She shrugged.

"You still mad at the Spanish?"

Phaedra sighed. "They was just protecting their own. Same as you wanted to protect that wee birdlet. Guess I shouldn't blame them for expecting us to pay for the freedom they offered. I reckon I knew the truth of it all along."

Chapter Thirty-Five

July 8, 1740

T he next day, Jem stopped to pick mulberries on the way to Mose. He gathered more than he could eat, thinking to share some with Phaedra. As he gazed at the dark stains the berries left on his hands, he thought about the oath to the Spanish king. Juba had given his last drop of blood for freedom.

What had Jem sacrificed? He thought about how things had changed since the moment cannonballs first shook the Castillo. Though he hadn't realized it at the time, by telling him about her bargain with Aunt Winnie, Phaedra had released him.

And she'd opened his eyes to something else. They'd kept their oath to the Spanish king. But it seemed to Jem there was another oath owed. Unspoken, but even more powerful.

He wanted to talk to Phaedra about it, but when he got to the patch of yard she'd cleared, the stump sat empty.

He called, but there was no answer.

He walked toward the place where he used to climb over the wall. Green shoots had already begun to peek out of the ashes and mud. Soon, grasses and vines would cover the burnt ruins.

Part of an old basket lay on the ground near the well. He picked it up. There were no burn marks on it. He held it to his nose and breathed in the sweet smell of fresh grass. It was new—half-formed and unraveling at the edges, as though the sweetgrass had decided it didn't feel right about being bent and bound into rows.

The sight chilled him.

Phaedra would never have left it lying on the ground like that.

Before he was conscious of what he was doing, Jem was running, hurtling over the fallen rubble of the huts, over the burned stumps that were once walls, over the trampled dagger plants, and through the cornfield. He sprinted into the forest, back to the place where he'd been attacked, where he'd met Juba and Adine, where he'd found Omen. Some part of him sensed he'd find Phaedra where it had all started.

When Jem got near the clearing, he slowed. Over the pounding in his ears and chest, he heard voices. He began to run again.

Up ahead, he could see her. And she wasn't alone. Phaedra was wrapped in the grip of a tall dark man.

Jem drew his knife and rushed forward, but the man must have heard his approach, for he pushed Phaedra behind him. She stumbled and fell. The stranger turned on Jem, hands fisted, eyes wild.

Though ragged and stained, the blue breeches he wore

looked somehow familiar. They were tight and had been cut off at the calf. Jem realized with a start that they were the ones stolen from Rojas.

"Leave off!" Phaedra cried. "He's just a boy!"

"Tell *him* to leave off! He's the one pointing the knife!"

Jem blinked. It didn't signify.

He faltered a bit, his steps slowed.

"What are you doing here, Jemmy?" Phaedra's voice was high and unsteady.

It took him by surprise, her calling him by that name. Suddenly, he was unsure. "You dropped your basket. I thought you—"

"This here is Cato," she said.

Jem looked at the man again and noticed the hide string around his neck.

A carved whistle dangled from the string. The first whistle Jem had made. The one he'd lost in the woods the night Juba and Adine arrived.

Realization closed his throat. His breath came shallow. "It was you!" he said. "You're the one who attacked me."

"No," Cato said.

"Liar! You have my whistle!" He had a sudden memory of the dark figure looming over him. "And now I remember seeing you."

"I saw it happen, it's true. But I wasn't me that attacked you."

"Who then?"

"It was a big hoot owl. That owl came down on you like a fury. I was hiding behind a tree and saw it. Tried to help you afterwards, but I heard someone coming."

"I don't believe you," Jem said. "Owls don't just attack folks."

"I swear it happened that way," he said. "Maybe she thought you were prey. Maybe you just got too close to her nest."

The tree. Omen's nest.

As he glared at the stolen whistle, he noticed it wasn't the only thing Cato wore around his neck. He also wore a medallion. An exact replica of the one Phaedra wore.

Jem felt dizzy. The air around him had become too thick to breathe.

"Cato's my husband," Phaedra said.

"Your…?" Jem shut his eyes. There was no sound but the beat of his blood pulsing in his ears. The wind held its breath and the birds had gone still. It was as though the whole forest waited.

"That's right," Cato said.

"But…if you're her husband, why didn't you come to Mose?

"Don't be a fool," Cato said. He held up his hands. The little finger of each was missing.

Jem's innards turned cold. "You're the one! You led the rebellion!" He looked at Phaedra. "Has he been hiding in the woods all these months?"

Cato said nothing. Phaedra bit her lip.

"Why didn't you tell me?" Jem said, but even as he spoke, he knew why she hadn't. He'd been so fixed on making himself feel important, so eager to prove himself worthy, he'd almost cost them their lives.

"We're leaving," Phaedra said.

"Where will you go?"

"Somewhere they won't find us."

Jem shuddered. "The Dismal?"

"Maybe," Cato said.

"I'll not tell anyone I saw you."

"You must," Phaedra said. "What happened at Stono is a truth needs telling."

"Don't let them believe we were drunken thieves," Cato said. "We'd planned that march for months. Down to the day and the hour. Planned it for a Sunday, when folks would be at church. Before the law said they'd have to carry guns there with them. We were coming south to take our freedom. Fight for it, if need be."

"What happened?" Jem said.

"Had it all worked out," Cato said, "Like Moses leading his people out of Egypt. Even the route we'd take to get here. When the day came, it started just as we'd planned. But as more men joined us, something turned. May have been something the shopkeeper said that set it off. I don't know. He was already dead when I got in there. By then the fire was burning strong.

"It was as though those flames ignited rage. It swept through our numbers, consumed us. The cry for freedom got choked. The mob wanted freedom, but they would also have revenge. When I look back on it now, I know it was in that moment we were lost. I stayed for a while. Tried to recall to the others what we were aiming for, but it was no use."

"What about Aunt Winnie?" Jem asked.

"She kept her promise." Phaedra put her hand on Cato's shoulder. "All this time, I believed him dead. Maybe that old woman has some kind of magic, after all."

"I thought you'd taken up with the little Spanish soldier," Cato told Phaedra. "I watched you from the woods. Either him or his girl followed you everywhere." He pointed at Jem. "I tried to talk to the boy, but he ran away every time I called to him."

"You never called me," Jem said.

Cato lifted the whistle to his lips and blew. "You can't tell the sound of your own whistle?"

Jem gaped at him. *The noise in the woods.* Then he had another thought. "Where's Aunt Winnie now?"

"In Charles Town. Wanted me to pass a message to you. She hoped you'd understand, but she never planned on coming south. Told you that just so you'd go on without her."

"Not coming?"

"Said it wouldn't be right. Too many folks up there need her," Cato said. "Best she stay put, she told me. But she said for you to be ready. She'll be sending others down to Mose. Wants you to look out for them."

Jem swallowed. "I will," he said. "I promise."

"We got to go," Cato told Phaedra.

She took two steps forward and grasped Jem's hands. A sparrow called, and another answered. "You turned out good," she said. "Did that old woman proud. Me too."

And then they were gone. Disappeared into the trees and shadows.

As he stared after them, Jem realized he was holding something.

He opened his fist.

There, its edges pressed into his palm, was Phaedra's medallion.

He gazed at the familiar image on the front for a moment, then turned it over. He'd never seen the other side. Etched into the silver was an image he knew from the catechism.

It was St. Christopher, the patron saint of travelers, a stooped figure with a walking cane.

On his back he carried a child.

Chapter Thirty-Six

October 14, 1740

The heat of summer had lifted, and the evenings turned cool. They were a small group around the fire: Jem, Big Sunday, Shadrack, and a few others. With lodgings spread around St. Augustine, they didn't gather every night, but came together as often as they could, usually near the north gate, closest to Mose. Domingo joined them most evenings, usually bringing a string of fish.

There were some new faces too. Every month or so, more arrived from the north. The slaveholders couldn't stop them.

Jem traced a finger along the beads in the hem of his shirt. Not because he believed they could protect him, but because they reminded him of Aunt Winnie and what she'd done for him.

Whooo, whooo, whooo!

He looked up from the fire, searching the sky.

"Omen?" Domingo sat down beside him.

The beat of the ka drum matched that of Jem's heart, strong and steady. He'd not seen Omen since he'd risen over the fire and flown free of the English. But Jem sensed he was out there, soaring through the night sky. "You still believe an owl is bad luck?" he asked Domingo, poking the fire with a stick. A burst of embers rose into the air.

"Not bad luck, just omen. Also, *tomo*." Domingo grinned at Jem's puzzled expression. "Means *guide*. My mother once told me owls are sent to guide us through dark places."

Jem studied on this and rubbed the medallion, warm and solid between his fingers. He thought of Phaedra somewhere in the darkness and wished for an owl to guide her. He could almost hear her voice. *Truth telling's what we need*, she'd said, *not tall tales*.

He would tell her story and Cato's. And he'd keep Aunt Winnie's stories alive. He knew now that the best tales, the ones that endured, told truths. But he also knew that truth could be as bendable as the grass Phaedra wove into her baskets. It could be gathered, twisted, and shaped to one's will. It took wisdom to separate the strands.

"I never got to hear the end of Aunt Winnie's story," Domingo said. "What happened after Brother Rabbit got the three impossible things?"

Jem smiled. He remembered Aunt Winnie's words as clearly as if she were standing there telling the story herself.

> *He laid them out for the Sky God and asked for the wisdom he'd been promised.*
>
> *"You're a clever rabbit," the Sky God said, "to have gotten the rattle of Snake, the tail of Fox, and the tooth of Bear. But cleverness is not the same as wisdom."*

Brother Rabbit leaned forward, eager for his reward.

"Although you have Bear's tooth, are not his claws the more powerful weapon? And Fox looks similar to Dog without his tail. How will you be able to recognize him in the woods? Finally, without his rattle, Snake will strike without warning."

Brother Rabbit scratched his ears. "What you say is true, Sky God, but I wouldn't call it wisdom."

The Sky God gazed down on him for a moment, then spoke. "Wisdom is this, Brother Rabbit: You'd best take care when you wander into the forest."

There was a moment of silence, then Domingo laughed. "Your aunt is a wise woman."

Jem smiled. It had taken him a long time to understand that everyone who'd gotten this far had ridden on the shoulders of those who'd suffered and sacrificed to make it so. No one could do it alone. That's where the stories came in. Like the ashes of the old fort tilled into the soil, the stories must be shared and passed on, so generations to come would rise even stronger. Jem would see to it. He owed it to Aunt Winnie and Phaedra, to Juba and all those who'd died fighting for freedom. Owed it to those still in chains, and to those like him who'd come searching for the other side of free.

Author's Note

THE OTHER SIDE OF FREE started with a relic: a hand-made silver medallion just under an inch in diameter, dug out of a marsh by an amateur archaeologist in the 1980s. You can see a photo of it on the Florida Museum of Natural History website and a replica in the museum at Fort Mose in St. Augustine. On one side is a mariner's compass rose. The other shows St. Christopher, patron saint of travelers. In the story, Phaedra wears it around her neck. I wanted to know who made the medallion, and who wore it.

I was inspired by the people of Fort Mose, who made a vow to a faraway king in exchange for their freedom. As well as converting to Catholicism, the escaped slaves pledged to "spill their last drop of blood" in defense of the Spanish King and to be the "most cruel enemies of the English."

While Jem and the other characters are fictitious, the story is based on historical record. Fort Mose was the first legally sanctioned free African settlement in what is now the United States. In 1994 the site was designated a National Historic Landmark and listed on the National Register of Historic Places. In 2009, the National Park Service named Fort Mose a precursor site on the National Underground Railroad Network to Freedom.

The people of Fort Mose made alliances with the Spaniards and their Indian allies and fought against their former masters. Records from South Carolina show that the English blamed the Spanish for the 1739 Stono Rebellion, claiming that the promise of freedom incited the rebels. It was to St. Augustine that the Stono rebels were headed when the uprising was suppressed.

Retribution was swift. Most of the rebels were executed within a month (though some evaded capture for six months and one participant remained a fugitive for the next three years). Oglethorpe led an attack and siege on St. Augustine in 1740. As in the story, the people of Mose and St. Augustine retreated into the Castillo de San Marcos (the largest and oldest masonry fort surviving in the United States). Fort Mose was captured and occupied by the English.

In a pre-dawn attack that took the English by surprise, the Mose militia and their Spanish and Indian allies retook the fort, burning it down in the process. But the siege did not end until shallow-draft Spanish ships evaded the English blockade and delivered supplies to the Castillo. With no hope of starving St. Augustine into capitulation, and the deadly winds of hurricane season fast approaching, the English retreated. Fort Mose was rebuilt in 1752 and occupied until Spain traded Florida to the English in 1763. At this time, the free Africans of Mose relocated to Cuba.

The St. Christopher medallion, dug out of the marsh over 250 years later, yields clues to a rich and storied past. The people of Fort Mose were among the first of the freedom fighters, proving that the battle to end slavery began many years before the abolitionist movement was organized. Fort Mose cast a far-reaching beacon of hope for enslaved Africans, and served as St. Augustine's first line of defense against English attack. For the people of Fort Mose, freedom was paid for with great effort and sacrifice. They are an important part of our history.

Bibliography

Arana, Luis Raphael and Albert Manucy. *The History of the Castillo de San Marcos, St. Augustine, FL.* St. Augustine: Historic Print & Map Company, 2005.

Austing, Ronald, and John B. Holt. *The World of the Great Horned Owl.* Philadelphia: Lippincott, 1966.

Berlin, Ira. *Many Thousands Gone: The First Two Centuries of Slavery in North America.* Cambridge: Belknap Press of Harvard University Press, 2000.

Bernd, Heinrich. *One Man's Owl.* Princeton: Princeton University Press, 1987.

Coakley, Joyce V. *Sweet grass Baskets and the Gullah Tradition.* Mount Pleasant: Arcadia Publishing, 2005.

Cohn, Michael and Michael K. H. Platzer. *Black Men of the Sea.* New York: Dodd, Mead & Company, 1978.

Deagan, Kathleen and Darcie MacMahon. *Fort Mose: Colonial America's Black Fortress of Freedom.* Gainesville: University Press of Florida, Florida Museum of Natural History, 1995.

Fett, Sharla. *Working Cures.* Chapel Hill: UNC Press, 2002.

Harman, Joyce E. *Trade and Privateering in Spanish Florida, 1732–1763.* Tuscaloosa: University of Alabama Press, 2004.

Henderson, Ann L. and Gary R. Mormino, editors. *Spanish Pathways in Florida.* Sarasota: Pineapple Press, 1991.

Hoffer, Peter Charles. *Cry Liberty: The Great Stono River Slave Rebellion of 1739.* Oxford: Oxford University Press, 2012.

Hurston, Zora Neale. *Mules and Men.* Philadelphia: J. B. Lippincott & Co., 1935.

Jones, Maxine D. and Kevin McCarthy. *African Americans in Florida.* Sarasota: Pineapple Press, 1993.

Joyner, Charles. *Down by the Riverside: A South Carolina Slave Community.* Chicago: University of Illinois Press, 1984.

Landers, Jane. *Black Society in Spanish Florida.* Urbana: University of Illinois Press, 1999.

Landers, Jane. *Fort Mose: Gracia Real de Santa Teresa de Mose: A Free Black Town in Spanish Colonial Florida.* St. Augustine: St. Augustine Historical Society, 1992.

Long, Carolyn Morrow. *Spiritual Merchants: Religion, Magic and Commerce.* Knoxville: The University of Tennessee Press, 2001.

Manucy, Albert. *The Houses of St. Augustine 1565–1821.* Gainesville: University of Florida Press, 1992.

McDermott, Gerald. *Zomo the Rabbit: A Trickster Tale from West Africa.* New York: Harcourt Brace & Co., 1996.

Milanich, Jerald T. *Florida's Indians from Ancient Times to the Present.* Gainesville: University of Florida Press, 1998.

Morgan, Philip D. *Slave Counterpoint: Black Culture in the Eighteenth-Century Chesapeake & Low Country.* Chapel Hill: University of North Carolina Press, 1991.

O'Brien, Stacey. *Wesley the Owl: The Remarkable Love Story of an Owl and His Girl.* New York: Free Press, 2008.

Parry-Jones, Jemima. *Understanding Owls.* Newton Abbot, 1998.

Smith, Mark. *Stono: Documenting and Interpreting a Southern Slave Revolt.* Columbia: University of South Carolina Press, 2005.

Topping, Aileen Moore, editor. *An Impartial Account of the Late Expedition Against St. Augustine Under General Oglethorpe,* A facsimile reproduction of the 1742 edition with an introduction and indexes by Aileen Moore Topping. Gainesville: University Presses of Florida, 1978.

Turner, Glennette Tilley. *Fort Mose and the Story of the Man Who Built the First Free Black Settlement in Colonial America.* New York: Abrams Books For Young Readers, 2010.

Waterbury, Jean Parker, editor. *The Oldest City: St. Augustine Saga of Survival.* St. Augustine: St. Augustine Historical Society, 1983.

Wood, Peter. *Black Majority.* New York: Norton & Company, 1974.

Glossary

atlatl: A tool for throwing a spear farther

chosa: A hut made of natural materials (from Spanish)

conjuration: A practice of magic that employs charms, spirits, herbs, and rituals

conjure bag: A small bag of charms for casting spells or warding off evil; it can be worn or carried

coquina: A limestone formed from broken shells and corals, often used for building

fire steel: A piece of steel used for sparking fire

gunflint: A hard stone that provides the igniting spark in a flintlock weapon

ka **drum:** An instrument with roots in West African culture used for entertainment, communication, and rituals

maroon: A fugitive black slave

obia: A monster in West African folklore

pirogue: A small boat

privy: An outdoor toilet

sally port: A gate or passageway in a fort used by troops going out to battle

smudge pit: A shallow hole in the ground filled with slowly burning plant material, used for smoking animal hides and keeping bugs away

tabby: A mixture of lime, shells, and water that becomes hard as rock when dry

teijami: A West African ceremony for helping the spirit of a dead person cross over into the next world

tomo: Guide (from the Timucua Indian language)

tricorn hat: A three-cornered men's hat that was popular in the seventeenth and eighteenth centuries

yaba: Omen (from the Timucua Indian language)